Kevin
and
KatheRINe
in the
Next
Lifetime

Kevin *and* KatheRINe *in the* Next Lifetime

CRYSTAL CHARLOTTE (CC) LANE

ARCHWAY
PUBLISHING

This is a work of fiction. All of the characters, names, incidents,
organizations, and dialogue in this novel are either the products
of the author's imagination or are used fictitiously.

Archway Publishing books may be ordered through booksellers or by contacting:

Archway Publishing
1663 Liberty Drive
Bloomington, IN 47403
www.archwaypublishing.com
844-669-3957

ISBN: 978-1-6657-5722-5 (sc)
ISBN: 978-1-6657-5724-9 (hc)
ISBN: 978-1-6657-5723-2 (e)

Library of Congress Control Number: 2024904046

Print information available on the last page.

Archway Publishing rev. date: 03/06/2024

Contents

Day 1.
The First Meeting in Fifteen Years

Day 2.
Settling in Together

Day 3.
Getting to Know the Island and Its People

Day 4.
Morning at the Pool

Day 5.
Kevin's Changing Mood

Day 6.
The Storm

Day 7.
After the Storm

Day 8.
The Art Gallery

Day 9:
The Cat Suit

Day 10.
The Assault

Day 11.
Ferry Ride to Maui

Day 12.
The Last Day

The Past to Their Future

Characters

Katherine (Rin)
Robert (Rin's first husband)
Kevin
Sarah (Kevin's wife)
Kai (little boy on Island)
Malia (Kai's mother)
Chioma (Rin's friend)
Rinda Blu (Rin's daughter)
Brian (Kevin's oldest son)
George and Phillis (older couple)
Daniel (Rin's second husband)
Sam and Jennie (Maui friends)
Brad (Art Gallery owner)
Dr. Shaw (Kevin's new friend on island)

*Rin Travels
to the Island,
Her Thoughts*

Rin Settles in for Flight to Lanai

As Rin settled in for her long flight to Lanai, Hawaii, to meet Kevin, she recalled some of their past together. They had an on-and-off affair for ten years, but for the last fifteen years, they hadn't seen each other in person. They kept in contact by phone and text messages nearly every week, sometimes every day, and even sometimes all day long back and forth, with short texts and phone calls, when time permitted. She had to see him just one more time. The break had been her decision, and she needed to lay eyes on him to make sure he was okay and could deal with the decision she had made; she was making it for them both.

They knew everything about each other's lives, whether it be doctor's appointments, dentist appointments, surgeries, spouses, families, and more. They discussed the births of their children and recent grandchildren and shared pictures. They discussed their careers, quite often giving each other advice. Rin often assigned lawyers from her firm to assist him with various projects, but she was never involved in person. She would not see him; she refused to see him, although she also shared nearly naked pictures of herself with him; she trusted Kevin and wanted him to know she was still in good shape, with a few extra pounds, of course. But because of her height, she carried it well. She was still that caramel-colored girl he loved so much. Although Kevin sent pictures of his children and grandchildren, he never sent pictures of himself. He said he was too old and had gotten too fat and didn't take good pictures anymore.

They kept up with the painful deaths of their parents and consoled each other through the grief. They knew each other's allergies, aches, pains, troubles, and sorrows; they knew each other's deepest secrets, wants, and desires. They talked about old friends and colleagues. And they often talked about the times they had together, their intimacies in exceptional detail, as well as the fun times with each other. Those intimate discussions sometimes led to phone sex or just a beautiful recollection of what it was like to be together. Rin loved Kevin then, and she loved him now.

They understood there would never be anyone else in their lives to make them feel the way they do with each other and about each other. Their times together, then and now, were hot, wet, intense, sensual, and passionate; there was more love shared than should be allowed between two humans. It felt like God made them for each other, but they somehow missed the opportunity the Lord gave them. They always expressed their love for one other after each phone call. Either it was a deep "I love you" or just "Love ya, babe," "Love ya, sweetheart, talk soon."

This went on for fifteen years. Not seeing each other was often unbearable, but they were true to their spouses and would not disrupt the lives they built with them.

No one knew about this relationship; Rin often wondered how she would know if something happened to Kevin in real time. How would he know if something happened to her? It would take time for either of them to find out; it could be weeks or even months before it got back to either of them something had happened. It was horrible to think that way, but deep in her mind, she would always know about Kevin. She would know. But she also knew they couldn't go on living this way. The relationship would have to end.

Rin ordered a drink to help her relax. She was quite anxious about seeing Kevin and even wondered whether he would travel all that way to meet her. She knew he loved her, but everything about their relationship was beyond complicated. The drink only brought her into deeper thought about their past.

Chapter 2

Rin and Kevin; Their First Encounter

R in recalled how they first met and what she felt for him at first sight. She couldn't describe those feelings to anyone else but only within her own mind, so she got comfortable and went into deep thought about those moments and spoke those most intimate feelings and desires to herself in silence. She had done this over and over throughout the years.

The first time I saw him, I thought, "Oooh, my goodness, what a beautiful man." I was not surprised at myself to notice how handsome he was; handsome is handsome, cute is cute, but I was surprised at myself as to how much I was attracted to him—an undeniable attraction that quickly included grave interest and an affinity of emotion and desire. For God's sake, I thought, he is a white man; and he is not my type. I liked tall, dark-skinned black men with pretty white teeth. And close shaven, maybe a mustache and well-kept beard, depending on the man and his individual look.

There was no doubt I had a type. My friends and family teased me about it all the time. Denzel Washington, Idris Elba, Morris Chestnut, and Richard Roundtree were my types. Truly handsome, dark-skinned black men that make you blush and weak in the knees. And now here he is. Who is this white man passing me in the hallway? Who is this gorgeous, tall white boy with thick blond hair, feathered back from his face? He had fair skin, clean shaven, and beautiful (but not my type) ocean-blue almond-shaped eyes. And there was that square jaw, broad, muscular shoulders, huge thighs, and rocking ass. And it was easy to notice all this about him, even with his clothes on. He was something to see. And what is happening with me? He reminded me of a hero in an action movie.

She smiled at herself for such a girlish thought.

We locked eyes for a second, so I think he noticed me briefly, and I thought I would melt away right there. His eyes—oooh, those eyes—and for that very brief moment in time, I could have gotten lost in those beautiful blue eyes. I never even noticed blue-eyed people before. His face and marvelous blue eyes reminded me of Ricky Nelson. So I did a 180-degree turn as he passed by, to keep myself afloat. Something I had never done in my life regarding any man; turn around to take that second look? It sounds cheesy to even think this way now, but as we passed each other, it was like a jolt of electricity or lightning that grazed my heart. I thought, "Oh well, that was that," and so I gathered myself, steadied myself, and headed to the elevator. I had a meeting on the thirtieth floor. I shook away the encounter so I could go on with my day.

And then this beautiful man appeared out of nowhere on that elevator with me. He put his hand inside to stop the door from closing and walked in, apologizing for his abruptness. I got to see him up close and personal, be near him. I looked up at him. He seemed seven feet tall as he stared down at me. But in reality, he was about six feet, two inches tall. Not much taller than me in my high heels. He made some small talk, but I didn't hear half of what he said. I was nervous, and my stomach did somersaults as it filled up with butterflies. Another new feeling I had never had about a man—at least not to this crazy extent.

Rin squirmed in her chair as she looked out the plane window and continued with her thoughts.

This man reminded me of the male leads in the old movies Mom and I watched, movies from the golden age of Hollywood in the 1930s and 1940s. I loved those movies, and I still do. It is the best way to spend a Sunday afternoon. He was a combination of Fred McMurray, Henry Fonda, Cary Grant, Clark Gable, Randolph Scott, Humphrey Bogart, and Errol Flynn. I couldn't choose just one; he reminded me of them all. But for the first time in my life, I was speechless and didn't know what to say. I was not, however, shy about looking at him.

I noticed he had a very symmetrical face, narrow waist, and V-shape torso with an overwhelming aura of masculinity, although he wore no cologne. He smelled naturally fresh and looked extremely fit up close. But there was a kindness and softness about him as well. And he smiled at me when he spoke, such a wonderful smile. He was neatly dressed in a crisp white shirt tucked into freshly ironed blue jeans with tan shoes and tan belt, and the top button of his shirt was open. It was about 70 degrees and sunny that day, so he wore no jacket. This white boy had me flustered and confused about my own wants and desires; I was confused about everything. No encounter with any man had ever made me feel this way. And a white man, at that.

Chapter 3

Elevator Ride to 30th Floor

R in spoke further to herself as she closed her eyes and sighed. The thirtieth floor was the top floor. I was surprised when he didn't get off when we reached my floor. I assumed that was his destination when he didn't press the button for any other floor. Very strange, I thought. Then it dawned on me he was interested in me; he wanted to know who I was. He asked my name and what I did for a living. After I answered, he didn't ask for my number, and I wondered why not. I noticed he pressed the lobby button when I got off the elevator. He just wanted to ride up the elevator with me.

I guess this was his way of having a conversation. As it happened, no one got on or off during that entire ride. After we parted, I couldn't stop thinking about him the rest of the day. He was even on my mind when I went to bed that night. I just couldn't get this white boy out of my head. What was his name? Oh yes, Kevin. Like Kevin Costner. I'll remember Kevin for a while.

Rin recalled shaking off the encounter with Kevin after the elevator door closed. She looked at her wristwatch. She was always on time, which meant she was at least fifteen minutes early. Rin was never late; that was her style, and she was building her reputation on it.

I settled in for that night after meeting Kevin and remembered thinking, "This is so silly. I have a wonderful man in my life, and Robert loves me very much. He's a handsome black man, successful, and good to me, and he'll probably ask me to marry him this weekend. And, I plan to say yes to his proposal." But Robert had never made me feel this way. I didn't even know it was possible to feel this way about any man. I wondered what was wrong with me. I found myself wanting to know Kevin, be with him, be near him again. He took over my mind constantly from the moment I first saw him.

Rin shifted her body because of the restlessness she felt just thinking about Kevin, and she remembered her final thoughts that day as butterflies continued those relentless somersaults in her stomach.

Well, at least I'll never see him again, I thought. And he will soon be out of my mind in time. I'll start the day fresh tomorrow, and this encounter will soon become a pleasant but very confusing memory.

But then that tomorrow came, and they met again by a remarkable coincidence.

Chapter 4

Rin Can't Stop Thinking About Him

Rin was a young contract lawyer back then and soon became engaged to Robert (who was also an attorney) shortly after her encounter with Kevin. Long before she met Kevin, she thought about all those times her girlfriends went out for drinks and dinner, and the subject of relationships came up: what they were going through with men, who they were dating, and so on. There were conversations about dating outside their race as well, when one of her friends talked about dating a white man she met.

Rin recalled saying, "Girl, please. A white man can't do anything for me; I'm just not attracted to them. I could never date one."

They all laughed.

Rin went on to say, "I'm not even attracted to those light-skinned brothers with curly hair. I like my men to have dark skin with pretty white teeth."

One of her friends replied, "Well, never say never, girl."

Rin thought that was such a long time ago, and look where she is now. What would her friends say now if they knew what happened years ago with Kevin, and the predicament she's in now? What advice would they have given her back then? Should she have told them? Some of them are still her friends today, but she just couldn't tell them about Kevin. She then acknowledged to herself that all her life, whatever she was going through, she kept it close to heart until she could decide on her own; the decisions she made about her personal life were her very own. Then there was no one else to blame for the outcome but herself.

That morning when the new day began, Rin had come out of the fog that Kevin had left her in and recalled a little more about the elevator conversation. Why was she still thinking about this white boy? She remembered telling him her name was Katherine. She never referred to herself as Kat, Kate, or Katie, as others did. She liked her full name, until later, when Kevin, the man she fell in love with, began to call her *Rin*. She loved the name Rin with all her heart.

As the elevator door began to open and just before she got off the elevator, she somewhat flirtatiously asked the man, "So what is your name?"

He said, "My name is Kevin, and it's very nice to meet you, Katherine."

"Nice to meet you too, Kevin."

He touched the down button for the first floor and said, "Hope to see you again, Katherine," as the elevator door closed.

Again, Rin thought, *The pretty white man showed a little interest in her, a black woman,* as she smiled. But even though she was making a joke to herself that morning, there was something about this man with the ocean blue eyes and blond hair. There was a connection, indeed; she still had those butterflies. It made no sense.

For some reason, Rin never told anyone about the encounter; she never expected to see him again, but she thought about Kevin most of the day. The very next day, another meeting was scheduled with the same client; it was odd that a second meeting was called so quickly. It turned out that the good-looking white guy (Kevin) was in the same meeting. He was a commercial developer, and they had the same client. She didn't realize just how truly handsome he was until he stood up to greet her; she wore flats that day, and he just towered over her.

"Nice to see you again, Katherine," he said.

She just nodded. When he shook hands, he held it a little longer than expected. He looked very serious but managed to smile. He made her a little nervous. She didn't know why; she'd done business with white men before, but this time, she was really nervous. When he held on to her hand longer than he should, it was almost like he read her mind.

Kevin apologized for staring and said he didn't know why he did that. "That was inappropriate," he said. "Please forgive me."

Rin indicated all was forgiven and smiled, while looking directly into his beautiful blue eyes.

Chapter 5

Working Together; Then It Begins

They found themselves working together quite a bit, and Rin started to have feelings for Kevin. Deep and growing feelings. He hadn't made a pass or given her any reason to think he was interested in her that way, but the feelings for Kevin kept coming; they kept growing. One day, as they were walking back to their cars, Rin mentioned she had a dream about him. She didn't mean to say it out loud; it just came out.

Kevin perked up and asked her repeatedly what the dream was about.

She said, "Oh, no, Kevin, nothing like that; it was just a dream about work, nothing more."

"I don't believe you," he said. "What was the dream about, Rin?"

She said, "Why did you call me Rin?"

"I don't know; it just came out: Rin. You look like a *Rin* to me. It has great meaning in the Japanese culture. That's what I'll call you from now on, Rin. I've been thinking about calling you that for a long time. Everyone else calls you Kat, Kate, or Katie. I wanted to have my own name for you."

Rin said, "I really like it. I like it very much."

Kevin finally stopped pestering her about having a dream about him. He closed her car door, and they went their separate ways. But the next day at work, he asked her about that dream again; he just wouldn't let it go. She finally confessed the dream was about a connection she felt they had, a special friendship and attraction. Apparently, he had been thinking about her a lot before that conversation; he had many dreams and thoughts about Rin, and it was more than a friendship. He just needed her to say something about how she felt. And so it began.

The next couple of days, they found themselves having lunch with other colleagues and noticed they were the only two left at the table; everyone had returned to their office or went to a meeting. Kevin and Rin had commitments as well but wanted to stay a little longer to visit with each other. There was always that need to be together somehow.

Finally, at the end of the third day, Kevin walked Rin to her car; it was a sunny, bright beautiful day, with lots of comings and goings of people and cars in the parking lot. They were standing at her car door, just talking. And suddenly and with no warning, Kevin kissed her. It was a long, slow, passionate kiss that nearly brought her to her knees. That kiss was warm, soft, and romantic, and brought even stronger desires that boosted her emotions and feelings for him. He put his hands in her hair and then just kissed her lips tenderly. It just happened, but it was the best kiss of Rin's life; the sexual desire she felt for Kevin was unbearable. It became an ache that he would have to satisfy.

Kevin said nothing after the kiss was over. He just opened the car door, and she got in the car to drive off, but couldn't. She was nearly paralyzed. He stood watching her for a second.

"Are you okay, Rin?"

She said, "Yes, of course, just need a minute."

She just sat there to regain her composure, but she didn't want Kevin to know the affect he had on her. She never thought about the hundreds of people who could have seen that kiss. She didn't care. He made her feel wonderful, just absolutely wonderful. It was a new feeling, one she had never felt before after a kiss.

Chapter 6

The First Time

As the intensity of their emotional and sexual attraction increased, they eventually started to make arrangements to be together as often as they could, whether they had sex or not. They couldn't get enough of each other's bodies, minds, and conversations. Even the arguments were worth being with each other. Their love life was the most beautiful part of her being alive. She recalled every touch, every encounter, what it felt like when he was inside her. It made her squirm just to think about him. It made her ache for his touch.

Rin thought about breaking off her engagement, but she couldn't, not for Kevin. He never gave her any indication he wanted her too. Later, she would find out he didn't know he had that option. The whole black-white thing, she thought he wanted to keep it a secret. But throughout the years, they discussed how much they wished they had made different choices so they could be together. The different worlds they discussed back then didn't seem so important anymore. But now (in this time), what's important is not to hurt the ones they love.

Rin went on to recall the first time they made love. She felt guilty because she was engaged. They secured a room in an upscale hotel early one morning, when they both should have been at work. It was the most beautiful experience she could imagine. It was magic. It started out as a hunger for each other, a need to relieve an ache for their desire. But it began to slow down tenderly and naturally, as Kevin removed her clothes and then his. They were still standing when Rin felt him and realized he was huge. She looked down to see. Her first thought was, *This white man has a huge dick*. She had felt him before, but never naked, and didn't realize the extent of his size.

He was hard as a rock, and she whispered for the first time, "Skin over rock, baby, skin over rock." There was not a lot of foreplay (except kissing and touching) because they spent a lot of time doing that over many months. She needed him inside her. He laid her on the bed and stopped to just look at her.

Kevin said what he would go on to say many times: "Mother Nature and God himself spent a lot of time on you, Rin. You are so beautiful."

He lay on top of her and needed no help from Rin to find his way inside. He gasped when he entered and said, "My God, help me."

Rin groaned as he entered. His strokes were slow and easy, not wanting to hurt her; Kevin was a little conscious of his size. But she recalled later discussing it, and he claimed he wasn't big, laughing that he was an average white man. They immediately found each other's movement and became in sync with satisfying their rhythm of his strokes. Kevin came quicker than he wanted, he was too excited, but surely made up for it later that morning in every way he could. They lay together not saying much, but they both knew they couldn't give each other up. This was not a one-time thing.

Rin recalled a time when they were travelling together along with other colleagues; they had to get separate rooms, of course. She was still engaged and didn't want anyone to know, and it couldn't help Kevin's career to be with an engaged woman (an engaged black woman). Around midnight, there was a knock on her hotel room door; she knew it was Kevin. She was waiting for him. They didn't make love right away; they just enjoyed time alone, talking. But it led to more. That was the first night Rin told Kevin she loved him. She just said it. She didn't care if he felt the same way; she just wanted him to know. Maybe he would stop her from getting married, she thought. Kevin told her he loved her too. He loved her very much. She waited for him to tell her not to marry Robert, but he didn't. She would later find out he was waiting for her to say she wouldn't marry Robert, that she wanted him.

But each time they made love that night, it brought more intensity and passion for each other. Kevin had a way of making Rin nearly lose her mind when they were together. He stroked and caressed her breasts, making her nipples rock hard, and then fingered her and placed his tongue between her legs, finding the spot that made her insane. All those touches made her nuts, and his kisses before he went inside drove her crazy. She reciprocated by placing her tongue and mouth on every part of his body, kissing his lips and using her tongue to caress both the inside and outside of his lips. She loved going down on him, but there was no way to get all of him in her mouth. She found other ways to satisfy him. She just wanted to love Kevin in every way possible.

Chapter 7

You're Hurting Me

R in further recalled a time they were trying to break it off, cool things down. They were both married by this time and were still technically having an affair, although seeing each other less and less. He was at her office in the early morning to meet one of her colleagues. She had asked him to work with another attorney on this particular project. It would be better that way. Kevin wanted to cool things down, as well. When Rin arrived at her office early that morning, there were very few people there. She saw Kevin waiting for one of her colleagues, she smiled and kept walking. They hadn't seen much of each other in the last few months, and she didn't want to alert any attention to their relationship, especially since they had no meeting scheduled. The chemistry between them was too apparent. Although she knew a meeting was scheduled, she was surprised he was there an hour early. The office staff was familiar with Kevin; he was a premier client, so he was let in the back office area to wait for his appointment. Kevin nodded at her but seemed distant and moody.

Nevertheless, Rin kept walking to her corner office. A few

moments later, he showed up at her office door. He looked sad as he walked toward her desk. She stood up to give him a hug; he seemed to need one. But he grabbed her and started kissing her hard and rough. He pinned her hands and body up against a wall and grinded on her until it hurt. He squeezed her arms and thighs until they hurt as well, while at the same time pressing his lips against hers hard and shoving his tongue down her throat. Rin tried to hug him and calm him down, but he kept at it. He was different; she didn't know this man.

She cried out, "Kevin, stop! You're hurting me."

He stopped as quickly as he started. He caught himself and walked over to sit in the chair next to her desk.

She said, "Baby, what's wrong?"

Kevin said, "I need you, Rin; I really need you."

Again, she said, "What's wrong, baby? What can I do to help you?" She noticed the bulge in his pants. She closed her office door and unzipped his pants. He was so hard, he was miserable. Absolutely miserable.

Nearly in tears, Kevin said again, "I need you, baby." She started to go down on him.

He stopped her and whispered, "I need to be inside you, Rin. We've been apart much too long, and I need you."

Rin loved Kevin, and neither of them cared if they got caught at that moment; she wanted to satisfy him. Rin took off her panties, faced Kevin while she straddled him, and put him inside, slowly. He pushed upward so that all of him was inside her. She began to move a bit, but he stopped her.

"Rin, please don't move; don't move, baby. I need you with me."

Rin sat on him, without moving. He rested his head between her breasts, and she stroked his blond hair.

She kissed his cheeks, saying, "It's okay, baby. Everything is okay."

She noticed Kevin was nearly in tears while he held her down on top of him, he held her tight until he came. Before he let her go, He said, "I love you so much, Rin. I just don't know what to do anymore."

After he was finished, he said he was sorry, zipped his pants, and left. She felt horrible but felt more horrible for Kevin. He had no idea he had hurt her, and she didn't tell him. She called him later that day to see if he was okay, and he said he was but still sounded distant. She left work early to take a bath before Robert got home. She was sore and wanted to see how many bruises she had and where they were on her body. It took her a few days to get over the bruises he put on her arms and thighs, and the grind on her groin took weeks to recover from. She had never known a man to get that hard. It was unnatural, she thought. But again, she just couldn't tell Kevin he hurt her. It would destroy him. He spent their entire relationship, ten years, trying to protect her from something or the other, and to know that he hurt her himself would be devastating to him. Rin understood at this moment, it was time to stop seeing Kevin. It just had to stop.

Chapter 8

Kevin's Type

The plane ride to Lanai was long, but first class did provide many comforts. Rin couldn't concentrate on reading or even watch a movie. She thought maybe the solitaire game on her phone would help; she tried a few hands but got bored very quickly; at least she was comfortable in her chair and ready to eat a little something when the flight attendant came around.

But still, all she could think about was Kevin. He tried to slow things down himself many years ago; Rin believed something was going on with his wife, Sarah, and he needed to spend more time at home. Or maybe he was afraid if she found out about them, it would be difficult for her to recover. There was so much for Rin to think about; they had been together for twenty-five years in the most complicated relationship she had ever heard of.

Rin often spoke with Kevin about how their relationship would affect their spouses; they were not being fair to them. Rin was having a difficult time herself navigating things at home. There was no doubt, they wanted each other, they needed each other, they ached for each other's touch. They needed to share each other's thoughts and discuss their desires and plans and dreams for a life together.

But now, they truly had to stop. And Rin would be the one to do it this time. So, for the next fifteen years, they did not see each other; they just stayed in touch.

Rin tried to take her mind off Kevin, but her thoughts continued. She was fully aware of the type of women Kevin dated before he married Sarah. They attended various functions where he brought a date and Rin brought Robert, her fiancé. Kevin's dates were petite blondes, maybe a size 0 or size 2, the total opposite of Rin. She was, indeed, the total opposite of what he was used to.

Rin was never jealous, for some reason; she didn't know why she wasn't jealous. She just wasn't. She wanted Kevin to be happy. However, in the beginning of their relationship, she often felt she was a novelty, something new in his life, but not permanent. So, she didn't push a real public relationship, but she did love him and with all her heart. They both laughed and commented to each other many times about how their feelings would somehow go away as time went by, especially without seeing each other, but the feelings grew stronger. After all these years, they still loved each other deeply and more than ever.

Rin went on to recall more about their relationship and how they were compatible in every way; Kevin was so protective of her during those first ten years, and even through those fifteen years they did not see each other. He was always checking on this and checking on that, a silent protector, ensuring she was okay and was never put in a position to be harmed. He tended to watch the people around her and the reactions they had to her while never saying a word about it. She recalled him saying she was so beautiful, she was different, and she needed to be more aware of her surroundings.

"Not everyone is a good person, Rin," he would say.

He was absolutely right. Rin had a tendency not to pay attention to her surroundings at all; it was something that bothered Kevin fiercely. She knew he could not bear something happening to her.

Chapter 9

Kevin's Protective Nature

The flight attendant interrupted her thoughts for a moment to ask if she needed anything.

She shook her head no, smiled, and said, "Thank you."

Although she was nervous about seeing Kevin, she did feel relaxed and comfortable with her thoughts about him. She then noticed a young couple across from her; they seemed very much in love. She noticed them because they were an interracial couple. He was white, and she was Asian. She wondered if it was their honeymoon. The man reminded her of Kevin when he was about that age. The way he looked at her and seemed to have a protective instinct toward her. Rin picked that up immediately.

It reminded her of a particular incident regarding Kevin's protective instincts when it came to her. Many of her coworkers, clients, and staff gathered at a restaurant for happy hour after a long workday. Rin and Kevin had not yet had sex, but they had kissed by now and were making plans to be together real soon. She had gone to the bathroom to freshen up a bit; she didn't even realize that Kevin had noticed she was gone. A man followed her around the corner to the bathroom. Kevin must have seen him watching her. The man waited for her to come out of the bathroom and cornered Rin. He said he just wanted to talk to her and get to know her. It was obvious Rin was not interested; she told him so.

But the man was persistent. He even touched her wrist and tried to move toward the back door.

He said, "Let's go outside and talk. I just want to get to know you."

Kevin appeared from nowhere and simply said, "Katherine, the babysitter is ready to go home. We have to leave now." He spoke with all the confidence and authority of intimidation.

The man apologized and said, "I didn't know, man. I'm sorry. I didn't mean any harm."

Rin could have handled the situation, but she was impressed by the way Kevin de-escalated it without incident.

She smiled and said, "Okay, sweetheart; I guess it's time to go home."

She wondered how he knew the man followed her. She also recalled the times when they were in the car and Kevin was driving and had to stop suddenly. He always reached out to keep her from moving forward. There were so many times Kevin looked out for her that she couldn't count them all.

Rin smiled as she recalled when they both got cell phones; they were brand new in the 1970s but became commercially popular in the 1990s; how Kevin complained about how she was all consumed by hers. Rin tended to not watch where she was going when walking anyway: fumbling in one of her bags, doing anything else but paying attention in the moment. Cell phones made it much worse.

When they were together, he would pull her away from something harmful as she walked and just shake his head. And during those fifteen years of not seeing each other, whenever she mentioned she was driving somewhere unfamiliar, he'd map out a safe route for her and remind her to be aware of her surroundings. Rin was, indeed, known for her frequent car accidents and fender benders; she couldn't seem to keep her mind on one thing. Although Kevin was not overbearing with his concerns about her well-being, she got the feeling he was afraid something would happen to her.

So if Rin had not spoken with Kevin in a few days, he would text, "Is all good?"

She would text back "Yes, all good. What about you?"

He would say, "All good, babe."

She knew he was checking on her. As time went on, he always knew when she needed him. If she let him, he would have put her first in his life. But his job and family responsibilities were overwhelming for him. She had to ensure those things came first.

Chapter 10

The Petite Blond and the Dinner Party

As she gazed again upon the young interracial couple, she knew the black-and-white issue between them was the excuse. They were just scared because of how they were each raised. They were both taught that marrying outside of one's race wouldn't work. The problems their families would put them through would have been unbearable, and the disappointment they would cause would soon destroy them, even though most in society would not have had a problem with them deciding to be together. But today, she knew the decision they made so long ago was a stupid one. And she was sure Kevin knew it too; she was absolutely sure he knew they made a mistake. The connection between them was so strong and had grown stronger each and every day. Rin loved Kevin so much. He was an amazing man.

Rin's thoughts continued. She couldn't sleep during the plane ride; she was just too excited about seeing Kevin. She stood up and headed to the facility so she could stretch her legs. She came back to her seat and ordered another drink, hoping that would help her relax so she could sleep. But it didn't. She kept reflecting on her past with Kevin.

She recalled how when they were out together with others, people always put them together, whether they were sitting or standing next to each other or not. Strangers would ask Kevin, "Is that your wife? Is that your woman? You guys make a beautiful couple."

The attraction between them could be felt within the room, any room; people noticed it, they felt it. One night, they both had dates at a dinner party sponsored by a client, and the seating arrangements put Robert, Rin's fiancé, on one side of her and Kevin on the other. Next to Kevin was his date: a beautiful, petite blonde, as usual (she thought). Rin thought about how pretty she was but noticed how he never deviated from a specific type. Being with her should have opened that door.

The client's wife greeted everyone at the table and told Kevin and Rin what a lovely couple they made. Robert didn't hear the comment; he was engaged in conversation with the person next to him. However, Kevin's date heard it clearly. Rin wondered what that conversation would be like on the ride home. She smiled to herself.

As time went on, they realized how much in love they were. Rin didn't want to hurt Robert and didn't want to hold Kevin back from the life he deserved, the life his family wanted for him. She thought maybe Kevin would see someone else after she announced she was marrying Robert after such a long engagement. As she expected, Kevin eventually married Sarah, a beautiful petite blonde, the traditional stay-at-home type that looked pretty when he came home from work. This was what she believed he wanted in his life, Rin was sure. And the woman he chose, Rin believed was good for him. She was a lovely person. Sarah would make Kevin happy. At least she was hopeful Sarah made Kevin happy all these years.

Chapter 11

Rin's Pregnancy

Rin finally felt sleep take over, but before dropping off, she recalled a conversation with Kevin that made her angry. Before she married Robert, Kevin often commented on how independent she was. That should have been a compliment, but he went on to say she acted like she didn't need anyone and would only marry Robert because that was the thing to do. He was convenient for her lifestyle and goals. He didn't think she really loved Robert. He was right, but it made her angry when he made that comment. And she told him so; in fact, she let Kevin have it good. She wondered how he could say some of the most stupid things. And within these last fifteen years, he still said stupid stuff. She had to smile; it was part of his charm. Finally, she fell asleep.

When Rin awakened from her nap, her thoughts returned to Kevin. She married Robert long before Kevin decided to marry Sarah. She and Kevin did not speak for first two years after her wedding. Kevin called her many times, but she wouldn't take his call, even though she missed him terribly. It was the most difficult thing in her life to stay away from him. She made sure they didn't have the same clients, or another colleague would take point if they did.

When Rin was about seven months pregnant, she found herself in an elevator with Kevin once again. She was as pleased to see him as he was to see her.

He looked at her belly and smiled. "Seven months, huh?"

"How can you tell?" Rin asked.

Kevin replied, "I know my Rin. That's how you would look if that was my baby. Is it my baby?"

She laughed and replied, "Absolutely not, Kevin, unless I carried it for two years."

They both laughed and decided to have lunch and catch up.

The waitress who took their order said, "So when are you two expecting?"

Rin said, "In about two months; we hope it's a girl."

Kevin looked adoringly at Rin and said, "Yes, a girl who will be as beautiful as my wife." He told the waitress, "She still takes my breath away. Still."

The waitress responded, "You two are absolutely adorable."

Those feelings were still there for both of them, that undeniable connection they had, and they were still very much in love. After the waitress left, Kevin told Rin he was married now.

Rin had heard about it and said, "That's really good, sweetheart. I always wanted you to be happy."

"I am happy," he said, "as much as I can be without you. Your pregnancy has made you more beautiful, and I didn't think that was possible. That should be my baby. Rin, you must know how I felt about you, how I still feel about you. We should have gotten together, you know that."

Rin said, "But we didn't, and it's okay. I really didn't think I was your type, Kevin."

He responded, "My type? What are you saying? You were then,

you are now, you're everything to me, and always will be. I think about you every day, sometimes all day."

Rin said, "The same, sweetheart."

So they decided to stay in touch, no matter what.

Chapter 12

15 Years Later

After Rin had her baby, Kevin went to see her and the baby in the hospital, without telling her. He had to know how she was; he needed to know if she and her baby were okay. Six months or so following, they resumed their sexual relationship in secret, and for the next eight years, that is what they did, every chance they got. It was easy because they were working together again.

Rin started her own law firm during that time; it was small, with one partner and three associate attorneys, some administration people, an investigator, and so on. Kevin's development company was doing very well too. He had contracts with many of the major retail chains. Rin was so proud of him. They helped each other in their careers and complimented each other's efforts.

They often said, "If we had married, what a power couple we would be."

Things were getting heated again and out of control; they were surely headed down a rabbit hole, where nothing mattered but each other. Decisions would have to be made about their relationship.

They both decided they didn't want to hurt their families, so they stopped seeing each other, but kept in touch to make sure each other was okay. They reflected on the many occasions people assumed they were married. They wish that were the case. But they cared about their families too much to make that turn now.

So now, fifteen years had gone by, and Rin was headed to Lanai, Hawaii, to see Kevin. She suddenly worried; she was fifteen years older than the last time he saw her: a few lines in the face, and that size 8 is pretty tight in some styles. She's now buying a size 10 sometimes to be comfortable. She looked down and patted her stomach and did a little pinch to measure the fat. She even pulled out her compact mirror to check the visible lines on her face. All of a sudden, she became self-conscious. However, she did try her best to stay healthy and keep in shape. Kevin might notice those few extra pounds, but she doubted he would care.

Rin recalled so many of the wonderful moments she had with Kevin, especially enjoying recalling why he called her "Rin." *Rin* was part of the spelling of her name, so Kevin explained the meaning of it and pronounced every syllable very slowly. She proceeded to pronounce her own name softly and out loud, emphasizing every syllable (Kath-e-RINe), the way Kevin pronounced it that day.

Kevin worked in Japan as a project manager for a large firm that did commercial development, and he became fascinated by the Japanese culture. The name *Rin* is Japanese and means "dignified, serenity, bells, and beautiful." It has been around for centuries. The name Rin has a long history and has been used by many influential people throughout Japanese history and deeply embedded in Japanese culture. In Japanese folklore, the sound of a bell is believed to ward off evil spirits, bringing good luck and prosperity. Therefore, the name Rin holds a symbolic meaning of protection. Kevin explained his growing love for her, and by giving her the name Rin, it described her character, her beauty, her grace, and his prayers for her. it gave him peace for her protection. She was, indeed, his Rin.

After remembering what the name Rin meant to them both, she relaxed and took another nap before the plane landed.

She awakened to the announcement of the plane's descent. They would be landing in about fifteen minutes. She looked around at the excitement of the other passengers and gathered her things. It was truly a long flight, a rare nonstop flight. Rin paused a moment and bowed her head. Not to have another conversation with herself about Kevin, but to have a conversation with God.

She spoke softly and said, "Oh, my dear God, please forgive me and forgive Kevin. Dear Lord, I ask for your forgiveness this one last time. I now have overwhelming confidence that Kevin will be there, so please forgive him too. It's been wrong all these years, and we both know it. But I must see him this one last time. I just have to. If I don't, I feel I can't go on. God, please forgive me. It's a terrible feeling, like I could die if I didn't see him. After this, I promise you with all my heart, it will end. I will get right with you. Kevin will get right with you. We will not continue to commit this sin and jeopardize our hope to be with each other forever in the next lifetime. I will be strong for us both, with the strength I know you've given me. Thank you, God. Thank you."

She raised her head, wiped away the tears that welled up in her eyes, and then straightened her clothes and said again softly, "Thank you, Lord, for this forgiveness."

Day 1.
The First Meeting
in Fifteen Years

Chapter 13

Rin Had to See Kevin

Rin planned this twelve-day vacation for her and Kevin five months out to give them both plenty of time to schedule time away from their everyday lives and families. She just couldn't take it anymore, even though she was the one who said she never wanted to see him again in person; she would see him in the next lifetime. Kevin had all the travel details, but she wasn't absolutely sure he would show up. Let's face it; twelve days is a long time to be away from the day-to-day of one's responsibilities and commitments.

But Rin packed her bags anyway, said good bye to those who loved her most; and headed to Lanai. She was fifty-three years old and scared to death at what she was doing, but in her mind, she had no choice. She would go absolutely crazy if she didn't lay eyes on Kevin again, just once more. Her flight was scheduled to land first, and she would drive to the villa she rented for them on the beach.

She had hoped to get there long before Kevin to buy groceries and to make sure the villa was what it was supposed to be. The villa had a master bath and half-bath, a living room, and a kitchen area.

There was a deck outside the bedroom's patio doors. She hoped it would be clean and decorated.

She reviewed the photos from the brochure she printed from the website and checked the website again on her phone; pictures can sometimes be deceiving. She was nervous and excited but still not sure if Kevin would come. He seemed a little concerned about taking the trip.

Chapter 14

First Time in Person After 15 Years

After Rin landed, she secured the keys to the villa and rushed over to its location. When she opened the door, to her big surprise, Kevin was standing at the bay window, looking out at the view. He arrived early; he must have taken an earlier flight. She couldn't believe it. She hadn't seen him for nearly fifteen years. He was as gorgeous as ever. He had on khaki shorts and a navy-blue tank top and sandals. He looked a little older and a little heavier in all the right places, but absolutely beautiful with a close-cut gray beard and mustache. His thick blond hair had lightened and turned to a shining, silver grey, swept back in feathers the way he always wore it. His shoulders were still broad with those muscular arms she remembered, and what a beautiful butt he still had. He stood straight and tall as a giant, as he smiled at her with his signature square jaw.

Rin thought, *Oh, God. Was this man beautiful and wonderful because I love him? Or do I love him because he is beautiful and wonderful?* He looked like a king from some fairy tale; she felt silly for even thinking that.

In that moment, Rin could hear her own heart thumping, and she grew weak in the knees as Kevin gave her this intense gaze as she stood at the door. She was surprised to see him but somehow held her composure. Then she immediately thought, *What he must think of me*? She had not stopped to fix her makeup or comb her hair because she had not expected him so early. She wore some makeup, but a woman her age needed to repair and smooth it out a bit. She was devastated as to what she must have looked like for him to see her (in person) for the first time after all those years. She wore white linen cropped pants with a navy blue T-shirt. They were nearly dressed alike. Rin was not skinny; she was also a little heavier since the last time he saw her, but she still had that small waist, more than her share of breasts, and a cute butt (more than her share of that as well).

Kevin walked over to Rin, gave her big hug, and kissed her on the cheek.

She hugged him back, kissed him on the cheek as well, and said, "It's so good to see you, sweetheart."

She was nervous and not ready to call him *Baby*, in person, just yet. But she did say, "I missed you."

He asked her if she would like to get something to eat and drink before settling in. He must have sensed how nervous she was and thought maybe they should sit down somewhere together to just talk and catch up first. So they went exploring for a place that served dinner and drinks, and found something that seemed very nice just a block or two away.

After entering the restaurant, Rin told Kevin she was going to the ladies' room and would meet him at the table. She had been too nervous to use the bathroom at the villa and also wanted to repair her makeup and comb her hair. She was still dwelling on how she must have been a terrible sight for their reunion.

After doing the best she could with her makeup and hair, she left the ladies' room and headed toward Kevin. As she got closer, Rin found him talking with a beautiful blonde, at least twenty years younger than them. Rin smiled at Kevin and waved, just in case he hadn't noticed she was headed that way. It was cute to see him with such a beautiful woman flirting with him. For some reason, Rin was never jealous of women who flirted with Kevin.

However, this young woman seemed to be making herself comfortable, so Rin decided to walk over to them more quickly. When arriving at the table, the smile was still on Rin's face; she was almost laughing. The question to herself earlier about whether she loved him because he's beautiful and wonderful? Or is he beautiful and wonderful because she loved him? The answer to those questions were yes. It was obvious this young woman saw what she saw. Kevin was still the most handsome man she had ever seen.

Rin's other question was answered as well. How did she look to Kevin? She heard Kevin tell the young woman, "Do you see this lady coming toward us? That's my woman; I love her more than she will ever know, and she still takes my breath away after all these years."

After that, the young woman left in a huff. Rin laughed and then sat down across from Kevin.

Rin said, "You put it on a little thick, don't you think?"

Kevin said, "Babe, it's true. You still take my breath away. You're more beautiful than ever. I suggested we leave the villa and come out for dinner, because I needed to calm myself down. When you came through the door, I thought, *How could she be more gorgeous?* But you are; you're my Rin."

Rin enjoyed the smiles between them as they began to enjoy their dinner and drinks. Although they were always caught up on what was happening with their families, friends, and work, it was wonderful to talk about things in person in the intimate setting of dinner and drinks. It was very nice to be able to do that after all these years. Rin felt no guilt by being there, and she believed Kevin had no guilt as well.

Chapter 15

Baby Blue Nightie and Silver Pumps

After dinner, they walked back to the villa, saying little; they just enjoyed the island. They didn't hold hands (Kevin was generally not affectionate in public, even though it was safe to be so on the island), but he occasionally brushed her fingers with his and patted Rin on the bottom as they got closer to the villa.

Kevin started to unpack and said he was taking a shower; he motioned for Rin to join him but didn't actually ask her to do so. Rin had something else in mind.

After Kevin showered, he came out of the bathroom with a towel wrapped around his waist and said, "Your turn."

His body was amazing, and she felt a little shy about staring at him too long. She went into the bathroom with a small bag, wiped off all her makeup, brushed her teeth, showered, and shaved a little down there, the way Kevin liked it. She brushed her hair, so it hung long and straight down her back, but it was full because of the air's humidity. She wanted her body to be natural; she wore no nail polish, eyelashes, or anything like that. Kevin had a thing for natural beauty, if there is such a thing. So she did her best. She put on a sheer baby-blue nightie; blue was Rin's favorite color. It had a plunging neckline with a loosely fit tie at the waist and hit just below the knees. You could clearly see the outline of Rin's body; her breasts and nipples, her navel, and the hairs on her private parts gleamed through.

She also put on a pair of five-inch silver rhinestone pumps. There was a purpose to those pumps. Rin was five feet nine inches tall, and Kevin was six foot two. Those five-inch pumps would make her eye to eye and shoulder to shoulder when facing Kevin. Rin enjoyed being tall. And although Kevin's choice of women appeared to be much shorter and more petite, he loved her height as well. However, she didn't know what to expect when she left the bathroom. Would Kevin have the room dark? Would he already be in bed? Was she too old to show this much of her body in the light? She was nervous and didn't know how she would look to him. Maybe she looked stupid. Well, too late to turn back now, she thought.

When she entered the bedroom, Kevin had dimmed the lights and opened the patio door of the bedroom to let in the evening breeze. He was still in his towel and standing at the patio, looking out at the beautiful view.

When he saw Rin, he smiled, walked over to her, and said, "You are beautiful, babe; you're stunning."

He gave her that long, lingering, passionate kiss he gave her the very first time they kissed over twenty-five years ago in that parking lot. Rin remembered how much she loved and enjoyed Kevin's kisses. He cradled her face in his hands without touching any other part of her body as he continued to kiss her lips, cheeks, and neck. They were all slow kisses. He ran his fingers through her hair slowly and let it cascade down her back and shoulders. He always loved her hair.

Kevin stood eye to eye with Rin and loved the idea of her being that tall at that very particular moment; he looked down at those sexy rhinestone pumps to see the source of her height. Then he gently pressed his body up against hers, moving her butt toward him.

Rin could feel how hard he was through the towel he wore. It was effortless for their privates to meet because of the height she gave him. He began to touch her body by again running his fingers through her hair, caressing her face and neck, kissing her there, then moving his hands toward her breasts while lingering on her nipples (pinching them slightly) to make them hard and large, like he knew they would be when he touched her.

Kevin moved his hands downward to grab her butt to bring her closer to him again with a lingering grind, and then he released her so he could feel his way to massage that special spot between her legs as he inserted his fingers.

He whispered, "Do you still like this, my sweet Rin?"

As they stood close together, he slipped her nightie down over her shoulders to expose her breasts so he could put his mouth on them; he stayed there a while, using his tongue and lips to enlarge her nipples even more. Rin thought he remembered everything. Then he slid her nightie down farther and put his tongue on her navel as he squeezed her butt. He let her nightie drop to the floor, and she stood completely naked before him; he sat on the bed to spread her legs open and then placed his head on her crotch as he squeezed her close. He moved away to finger her some more, but Rin had already come several times and was completely wet and moist. She needed Kevin badly; she needed all of him. He stood up again and removed his towel as they held each other, naked, from top to bottom. Kevin continued his soft and sensual grind. He was so hard, she couldn't stand it. She moved with him in sync like there had been no lapse in time between them. They both still knew each other's bodies and how to move together for their ultimate satisfaction.

Rin was out of her mind by that time, and she wanted to show him that same kind of lovemaking. She stepped out of her nightie and slipped off her pumps. When she looked up at him, her breasts were buried in Kevin's chest, and the most sexually sensitive parts of their bodies still met. He just needed to bend his legs a little, as he gently squeezed her butt to bring her close for that grind. They kissed and kissed and kissed, and more kisses.

Rin whispered in Kevin's ear to sit on the bed. He again buried his face between her legs as he caressed and squeezed her butt. She leaned down and reached for him and grabbed him with her hands. He was so hard, like skin over rock, just like she remembered. His penis stood up like the Eiffel Tower as he sat on the side of the bed; he was huge. Rin remembered one other time when they made love in a chair at her office, when the same thing happened. It was an unusual hard-on; Kevin was long, thick, and hard. He was big.

She recalled that time he just needed to be close to her, when he was really rough, and it hurt when he grinded against her and the bruises that resulted from his aggressive touches; it took her days for the soreness to leave. To this day, she never told Kevin he hurt her, because he stopped immediately when he realized what he was doing. She remembered his tears and the sadness, and recalled that was the day she decided never to see him again. It was that same kind of hard that he had then, where he needed to come inside her; that was the only satisfaction she could give him.

Chapter 16

First Time After 15 Years

They had twelve days for extensive foreplay, so she knew he needed to be inside her right then; it had been a long time since they had been together. Rin caressed him a little longer with her hands, but what she really wanted to do was put her mouth on him, but that would have to wait. His groans had become intense. And she had already come herself; she was wet and moist. Kevin needed her badly, and she needed him just as much. She recalled all of his favorite positions; nothing had changed, she was sure, because they talked all the time. But tonight, they needed to feel close; tonight would be about more than sex. And for sure, they had time to experience it all again. The anticipation of him inside her made her come again.

Rin motioned him to sit farther back on the bed. She straddled him, facing him like she did in that chair many years ago. It was much easier this time because they were on the bed. She put him inside her and wrapped her legs around his waist. He pushed up to make sure she had all of him.

He whispered, "Don't move, Rin; please don't move, babe. I just need to feel you." He groaned with pleasure and told Rin how much he loved her and missed her. He continued, "I'm crazy about you. Babe, you are so hot and warm, just like I remembered. But please don't move, not just yet."

But what he meant was that being inside her made his penis hot, like it was on fire. She felt that warm and hot feeling herself. The first time he told her that, she thought he meant she looked pretty. Neither had that kind of experience with anyone else. Kevin was so big, all she could do was hold on to him for dear life; although it hurt a little, it had been a long time since she felt that good.

They held each other tight as he placed his head between her breasts. She stroked his hair and kissed his forehead, his ears, his shoulders: anything and everything she could reach with her mouth and tongue.

She used her tongue to give him a sensual feeling as she sat on top of him, as he whispered again and again, "Babe, please don't move, not yet."

When Kevin finally released his tight hold on her, Rin began to sway in movement with some up and down strokes. She slowly caressed his back and neck; they continued those sweet kisses. They found each other's rhythm, as they did in the past. Rin was so wet, the orgasms kept coming and coming. They were close again; they were together as one.

They needed that kind of closeness with each other; they were both very sexual with each other and always had been. They had always been good with each other when it came to passion and sex. When Kevin came, it wasn't just one moment of release; it kept coming.

He whispered, "Your pussy is still hot, babe. You are so warm and comforting to me. I remember how wet you can be. I needed you more than I knew. I'm so glad I came here to be with you."

She stayed on top of him for a few minutes longer after they both came, and they didn't say much after that.

She only responded, "I really missed you too."

She lay down under the sheets, and Kevin joined her, with Rin's butt up against him. Kevin rested his hands around her waist, just under her breasts, reaching upward from time to time to stroke her nipples. This was the way they always went to sleep together.

Chapter 17

This Is Real

Rin and Kevin weren't tired and didn't want to go to sleep that night, at least not right away. Even though it was close to midnight, and it had been a long travel day, they stayed up to talk. After discussing the day's travel and holding each other for a while longer, they got dressed and took a quick stroll down to the water. They decided to buy groceries after spotting an all-night convenience store. Rin knew they'd rather not go out in the morning, so they needed at least breakfast groceries for the villa.

Kevin noticed her loose-fitting cotton dress and asked Rin, "Do you have panties on under that dress?" He remembered she rarely wore underwear under such clothes, but he was disappointed when she said yes.

However, she made him laugh and even blush a little when she said, "Not only do I have on panties; I needed to put tissue down there, as well." She added, "There is no way I'm going to shower you away tonight, I want to stay nasty."

Kevin laughed as well, but he didn't blush this time. Rin always came up with some smart comments.

They returned to the villa and put the groceries away; they were both tired and decided to get some sleep. They were not in their twenties anymore, even though they may have forgotten that fact during that lovemaking session earlier that evening. Rin started to put on a cotton T-shirt to sleep in, but Kevin said he wanted her to sleep naked with him, something she had not done in a long time. Of course she had no problem with that; she laid her head on Kevin's shoulder but still couldn't sleep; she was too excited. She kept playing over in her mind their lovemaking only a few hours before.

Kevin couldn't sleep, either, and she noticed him getting hard again against her butt. She caressed him and put her mouth on him, sweetly and passionately, something she had wanted to do earlier in the evening. Kevin tousled her hair as she went down on him; he moaned several times and grabbed her hair tight, but not enough to hurt her.

Rin knew he just loved her long, jet-black hair, and there was a lot of it. He enjoyed running his fingers through it. She could tell he was about to come again because he stopped her and had her lay on her back. He opened her legs and began to go down on her.

She said, "Baby, I'm so nasty down there. I'm not only wet, but I still have you inside me."

He merely said, "I don't care," and down he went.

After she came again from the pure enjoyment of his tongue and fingers, Kevin climbed on top of her. He began those long strokes Rin remembered, where he would slowly pull out, so the tip of his penis was at the edge of her pussy, hold it there, and then slowly push back in. He did that several times and then began to speed up his strokes. She realized it didn't hurt anymore; it was all just pure pleasure and ecstasy.

He said, "Open your eyes, Rin. Look at me; please look at me, babe. We're here together; this is not a memory or fantasy. This is not phone sex. This is real."

Rin opened her eyes to look at Kevin; she looked straight into those beautiful blue eyes, as they were one. It was, indeed, real. It was beautiful.

Those long, slow strokes were one of those special ways Kevin made love to her. This was how he loved her that very first time. Just then, Kevin stopped so he wouldn't come yet; Rin knew he stopped to keep up his stamina to continue to satisfy her, but she was beyond satisfied. He always thought of her first when they were together: what would make her happy, what he could do to make her feel good. But Rin felt the same way about him, so she changed the rhythm and began moving faster, touching and squeezing his butt against her, to excite him so he had no choice but to speed up his strokes. He had no choice but to come. Their bodies always moved well together; they were always in sync with each other's sexual and emotional needs. Kevin came again for the second time that night.

Rin thought, *This is not your usual man at any age.*

Kevin asked Rin if she wanted to take another shower or change the sheets. They both had come so much, and the bed was wet.

Rin said, "Absolutely not. This is how we loved each other tonight. Let it stay the way it is."

Not long after that, they fell asleep while wrapped in each other's arms.

Day 2.
Settling in
Together

Chapter 18

Kevin Watches Rin While She Sleeps

Both Kevin and Rin were early risers and always had been; they knew that about each other in the very beginning of their relationship. It was one of the major things they had in common. But that morning, Kevin woke ahead of Rin and watched her sleep as the sun rose. The room soon became filled with bright sunlight. As the sunbeams slowly moved across her hair and the side of her face, Rin looked like an angel. She was half-black and half-Iranian, and her Persian genes gave her a striking and exotic look. It was hard to tell what nationality Rin was, but she was indeed African American.

Kevin always thought Rin was the most beautiful woman he had ever seen. Her mother looked like Dorothy Dandridge, the beautiful black actress who was famous in the 1950s. He saw a picture of her, a picture Rin proudly displayed. Kevin somewhat remembered the story of how her parents got together; Rin's father was Persian, and they were an interesting pair. They married, but they didn't stay together very long. He was some kind of rolling stone. But since they had made Rin, Kevin didn't care. Rin was more lovely and exquisite than ever with her caramel-colored skin with that thick, long, jet-black hair.

Her back was to him, so he moved the sheets down to look at her body. On her back he noticed a scar, an old scar; he hadn't noticed it years before, or he would have asked Rin about it. He checked out her arms and noticed a few burn marks. Knowing how clumsy Rin could be, she probably burned herself while cooking, but he would ask her about that as well. He moved his eyes down to her small waist and beautiful round butt he loved so much; it was attached to those beautiful caramel-colored thighs. Rin had long legs that seem to go on forever.

Rin must have felt cool while she slept. She pulled the covers up that Kevin had pulled down and turned to sleep on her back. He moved the hair away from her face to look at her further. He couldn't believe how young she looked, with no makeup. She was very pretty and didn't look like someone in her fifties.

Kevin thought, *Rin must think I'm an old man now, all this gray hair.*

Then he thought back to something Rin said before when she sent him some pictures: "Maybe I look good to you because you care for me." Kevin wondered if that could have really been the case. Could Rin be this beautiful because he loved her? That couldn't be it, he thought. He noticed how men were looking at her in the restaurant; even other women noticed how striking she was. Of course, Rin didn't notice a thing.

He moved the sheets downward to look at the front of Rin's body. He absolutely loved her breasts, especially those nipples. They were still round and full, even larger than he remembered. He thought, as he always did, God and Mother Nature spent a lot of time on Rin.

He wanted to touch her breasts that morning, put his mouth on her nipples, and watch them become as large as his thumb before his eyes in the sunlight. But he also didn't want to wake her, so he stared at them awhile. He put his hands on himself and began to feel himself become hard. But he still didn't want to wake her, so he refrained from touching her, as difficult as that was. Plus, he wasn't sure if he could start something he couldn't finish. Last night had, indeed, been a workout. He slowly moved the sheets down farther to look at Rin's private part and just smiled, and of course it made him harder.

So he touched himself again with a few small strokes. All he knew was he wanted to satisfy her each and every day they were together on this island: lovingly, sexually, and spiritually. She absolutely did take his breath away. Yes, she was real; this was real, and he loved her deeply. There was no doubt Rin was absolutely beautiful to him and everyone who saw her. As he continued to look at Rin while she slept, he had to remind himself to remember to breathe.

After staring at the love of his life for moments longer, Kevin decided to let Rin sleep, but as she got up, she woke and said, "You're up. I'm not surprised. After I take a shower, I'll make us some breakfast. But before I do all that, can we talk, sweetheart?"

Kevin nodded. "Sure, babe, what's up?"

She replied, "I plan to wash my hair and keep it natural while we're here on the island; it's much easier for me. There is too much humidity and too much water to keep it straight." Rin explained that she didn't want to go through the daily task of blow drying and flat ironing. That would be a lot of work to last only a short time. She further explained that her hair is what black folks called "in between" (in between white and black hair textures).

She continued, "I know you like it straight, baby, but my hair will fall into ringlets after it dries. I can leave it down, put it up, wear a ponytail, whatever you like. But I will not be straightening it on this trip. Is that okay with you?"

Rin did want to please Kevin with how she looked, but a line needed to be drawn in this regard. She added, "I know you've seen pictures of black women with their natural hair before, because I sent them to you. I sent you a picture of me with my hair natural as well. And you didn't like it at all. Remember? So what do you think now?"

Kevin was surprised by the whole conversation. He looked puzzled that they were even talking about black women's natural hair; he didn't care. He didn't even remember any previous conversations about it. But he wanted to be careful about what he said. He was definitely caught off guard by this whole conversation.

"You know, babe, please understand you are beautiful no matter what; whatever you do to your hair (or not) is all part of who you are and all part of your unique and exquisite beauty."

She smiled.

Kevin wiped his forehead and said, "Whew. Did I get that right, babe?"

She laughed nearly uncontrollably.

Rin motioned to get out of bed and decided to crawl over Kevin instead of getting out of bed on her side. As she did that, Kevin stopped her from getting up and put his finger inside her.

She said, "I'm nasty down there, baby."

But he fingered her some more and then put his fingers in his mouth and said, "Nasty never tasted this good."

Rin laughed and shoved her tongue in his mouth to get a taste for herself and then left for the bathroom. She sat on the toilet to pee, and Kevin came in to brush his teeth and shower as well.

She said, "No privacy, huh?"

Kevin nodded and answered, "Not on this trip, babe."

She got up from the toilet, brushed her teeth, and got into the shower. It was a large bathroom, with plenty of shower room, so Kevin joined her.

He said, "Babe, let me wash your hair."

Rin was surprised; it wasn't something she could never imagine Kevin doing, but he lathered her hair with sensual passion and then washed her body. He took the head of the shower and rinsed her hair and her body, spreading her legs and placing the shower head between them, to get rid of the nasty, as she called it. They laughed. Rin then washed Kevin; they kissed for a long time until the water ran cold. They did not have intercourse, but the intimacy of that shower was beyond wonderful. It had been many, many years since they showered together.

Chapter 19

Rin Meets Kai

Rin put on the cotton T-shirt she started to wear to bed the night before; it covered her body to the middle of her thighs. She wore nothing underneath it; it was a warm day, but they didn't want to turn on the air conditioning. They both decided the island breeze from the outside would cool them.

Kevin got dressed in shorts, no shirt, but took a tank top with him and headed out. He wanted to explore the island a bit, maybe even take a swim in the pool near the villa. He spoke with Rin earlier and learned she wanted to stay in until they got ready for their dinner date later in the afternoon; she would have breakfast ready when he returned. For now, Kevin could see she just wanted to relax from her trip to the island, since they planned to seek out music and dancing later that night.

While breakfast was cooking, Rin stepped outside the villa for a minute and met a little Hawaiian boy name Kai. He was a cute little boy with a missing tooth in front. He wasn't more than seven or eight years old. He was riding his bike past the villa as she was singing and placing flower vases on the porch. She found the vases in the villa and thought she would purchase flowers for them later that day.

It was summertime, so school was out. Kai stopped to hear Rin sing.

He said, "You have a pretty voice, and you're really tall. You're very pretty too."

She chuckled and said, "Why, thank you. My name is Ms. Katie; what's your name?"

He said, "Kai."

She said, "Well, Kai, where I come from, there are women as tall as I am and some taller, and they can surely sing a lot better than me."

Kai laughed and said, "You sing really good, Ms. Katie."

Rin asked Kai if he had breakfast. He said not yet, his mother was working that morning and would cook breakfast later.

Rin replied, "Well, Kai, breakfast is all done here; you're welcome to eat with me."

He said, "Sure."

Rin thought he was the cutest and kindest little boy she had ever met. As Kai ate breakfast, he asked all kinds of questions like children do, and after he finished eating, he asked if he could come back tomorrow.

Rin said, "You sure can. See you tomorrow, but please ask your mother if it's okay first."

"I will," Kai said and rode off on his bike.

Rin soon learned from Kai that he lived in a neighborhood near the villa, and his mother, Malia, worked for the company that rented out the villa units.

Chapter 20

The Wedding Rings

R in and Kevin didn't see Kai every morning for breakfast, but he joined them many times during their stay. Later that afternoon, Rin found where Kai's mother was working near their villa. She wanted to make sure it was okay for him to have breakfast with them from time to time. Malia said yes. Rin liked Malia and could tell she liked her as well. Rin made sure that she had an opportunity to meet Kevin; he stopped by to see Malia on his morning walk that very next day.

Kevin returned sometime later that morning (just after Kai left), and breakfast had gotten cold. Rin thought it was odd that he was gone longer than expected, but she really didn't care. They were on vacation, and there were no time constraints on vacation. However, Kevin's demeanor was a little strange and the conversation about what he did that morning was even stranger to Rin. He seemed to be shuffling his feet and looking downward.

Then he pulled out a set of wedding rings from his pocket. Nothing expensive, Rin thought; they were silver with glittery rhinestones. The rings were kind of pretty, though. However, she didn't pay that much attention to how the rings looked; her attention was on why he bought them in the first place.

Kevin asked her to wear the ring he bought for here when they went out. He planned to wear one as well.

"Wear these rings?" Rin echoed in surprise. "How odd, Kevin. This is not necessary, absolutely not necessary."

Kevin said, "Please do it, Rin, for me. Please."

Even though she thought it odd and even strange, she agreed. She placed the ring on her finger, and it fit perfectly.

"How did you know my ring size?" she asked.

Kevin replied, "I tried it on my pinky finger and figured it would fit you, that's all."

She said, "Oh, okay," and smiled slightly, but still thought it was strange and put the ring on the counter. She just chalked it up to one of those stupid things Kevin did sometimes.

Kevin walked away from Rin and went to wash up while Rin heated breakfast. In truth, he thought back to when he bought Rin an engagement ring many years ago; he always knew her ring size. He walked by that engagement ring at least ten times at Tiffany's and finally got up the courage to buy it for her. He was going to ask Rin not to marry Robert and to marry him instead.

Kevin recalled the first time he saw Rin wearing Robert's engagement ring. Rin and Kevin had met that Tuesday before the weekend she got engaged. When he saw her at a meeting they both attended the following Tuesday, she was wearing an engagement ring. He remembered how his heart sank when he saw it. He had only known her a week, but it hurt him tremendously when she confirmed she was engaged. He shook away that memory; it was too painful.

Chapter 21

Sex on the Kitchen Counter

After breakfast, they watched a little local television to get a better feel of the island; Kevin fell asleep, so Rin decided to clean the kitchen. She sang as she cleaned; she had a pretty good singing voice. Kevin awakened from the kitchen noise; after watching her a bit, he got up from the couch and grabbed her from behind. He had gotten hard watching her. He placed his fingers between her legs and found she was beginning to get wet and turned on by having him so close.

Rin said nothing while he moved her forward to bend over the kitchen counter, raised up her T-shirt and inserted himself inside her. It was an old-fashioned fuck from behind.

He said, "I love this ass, baby." He was going at it fast but gentle; it felt so good to them both. This was one of Kevin's favorite positions.

Rin could always tell when Kevin was about to come before he wanted to. He'd stop for a second, hold on to her, and then start up again.

This time, she cried out, "Please don't stop, baby; not this time. Please don't stop."

It was too good for her. He started up again fast and furious, and then he came. He was so looking forward to having sex from behind; Rin could tell. She turned to face him and give him a kiss and hug. He just grabbed her gently and held her like his life depended on it. Then he gave her that kiss she loved so much.

Chapter 22

Ensuring Rin's Safety on the Island

Later that afternoon, they got ready to go out for dinner and to hear some music; maybe they'd walk around or hire a driver to tour the island and find out about some of the activities. Kevin wore an off-white printed shirt and dark pants and sandals. Rin wore a black sundress trimmed in yellow with flat comfortable walking shoes. Her hair was piled loosely on top of her head for comfort as well. She wore a little makeup and lipstick.

Kevin asked her, "Where is the ring I asked you to wear when we go out?"

The ring was on the counter, and she retrieved it and placed it on her finger. But again, she said, "What's up with this ring thing, Kevin? Why is it so important to you?"

Kevin wanted people on the island to believe they were married. Rin could not understand why that mattered and asked him what difference it made.

"It matters to me, Rin; please just do it."

Kevin continued, "This is a small island, and there are not a lot of tourists; it can only cater to so many. The tourists here are young and old couples, and maybe some single women and men here and there, some gays, and some others. It's a safe place, no worries there. But I didn't see any black tourists, black women. While I was out exploring the island earlier today, people asked me about the beautiful black woman I was with. This island is like a small town; everyone sees everything. And some wondered who you were to me; both natives and tourists asked me about you, Rin. It's to my detriment that I didn't show intimacy in public when we first got here. I was even asked if you were my wife or girlfriend. She's a really beautiful lady, they would say. So I said you were my wife. I just blurted it out. I don't want anyone to think you're available to anyone but me. I think it would be safer that way."

Rin said, "Oh, please, Kevin. You might be over cautious here. And safer how? Like you said, the island seems safe enough. The worst that could happen is someone may flirt a little, and there is no harm in that."

"Maybe so, babe," Kevin responded with a little laugh, "but you're officially my wife as long as we're on this island."

Rin gave him a salute and said, "Okay, sir, as you wish."

She had no problem playing that wife role with Kevin; it reminded her of their past and how people thought they were married anyway. Sometimes, it was a lot of fun. But sometimes, it hurt, because of the wishful thinking behind it. And just maybe this was part of Kevin's fantasy while they were together on this island, and nothing more.

Chapter 23

Dinner, Dancing, and the Booth

They found a restaurant that played music from the 1970s: just what they wanted to hear. They had dinner, drank a little more than they should have, danced, and had an amazing time. She loved to dance with Kevin. But when she first met him, he had no rhythm at all. So she had to teach him to dance. But now, he could step better than any brother out there. Black girls were in awe when they saw Kevin dance. The restaurant was outside on sand near the water, and when it got dark, there was intimate lighting. After dancing most of the night, Kevin and Rin sat down at their booth to catch their breath. They weren't in their twenties anymore but surely held their own with the young people there. So they sat and drank more, relaxed, and watched others dance and have fun as well.

As they sat next to each other in the booth, Kevin leaned over to Rin and whispered, "Do you have panties on?"

She laughed; that seemed to be his standard line on this island. "No, I don't, should I?"

She laughed again. She sat on the inside, and Kevin was on the outside of the booth. It was dark enough for him to place his hands under her dress without anyone noticing. He didn't finger her; he just massaged her the way he would sometimes do in their past when she was turned on. Rin opened her legs wider so he could then place his fingers inside; she groaned just a bit. At the same time, she put her hands on him as well; he grew larger and larger. She giggled when he started to squirm; the bigger he got, the more uncomfortable he was in his pants.

She whispered, "You started it." They acted like teenagers, and it was fun.

They left shortly after to go back to the villa. Kevin kept his arms around Rin during the walk home. They didn't say much, just enjoyed the walk and the island view. When they got back home, they showered quickly to get some of the sweat and sand off their bodies, got in bed, and assumed the position where Rin would back herself into Kevin; he would hold her while they slept. Kevin loved to sleep with Rin's butt up against him. She had already came at the restaurant. She believed Kevin came a little as well, but he didn't say. Anyway, they were tired, drunk, and sleepy.

Day 3.
Getting to Know
the Island and
Its People

Chapter 24

About Lanai

Rin wanted this day to be a day of adventure. No intense lovemaking this morning, just playful kissing and fondling; she wanted to get out early to really explore the commercial section of Lanai City. She knew she and Kevin had a special bond that transcended the physical and emotional. They had this time to live together, away from worries and away from the day-to-day grind of just living. They had reconnected physically and got comfortable with living together, even for this short time. It was old times, but much, much better; no hiding their feelings for each other on this island.

During breakfast, Kai joined Kevin and Rin just for a quick bite; he had plans to play with some of his friends. After breakfast, Rin put a cream-colored sundress over her swimsuit, while Kevin wore long swim trunks and a coral tank top. They took a boat ride around the island and saw such wondrous sites and the most beautiful humpback whales. There were also Hawaiian monk seals, an endangered species; *honu*, green sea turtles; mouflon sheep; and axis deer.

The boat docked at a port for more sightseeing and shopping.

Rin brought a colorful, boho cross-body bag to hold whatever she purchased, plus a blanket, snacks, and water. Kevin often had to carry that bag, and he absolutely hated it. It looked to girly for him, but he carried it anyway, whenever it got heavy and Rin asked.

They found that untouched Lanai has few paved roads, no crowds, and lots of space to unplug and let the island's slower pace of life soothe their souls. They explored the historic town of Lanai City, which was a short ride from the harbor where the boat was docked. They discovered quaint shops and an array of restaurants, art galleries, and a newly renovated historic movie theatre. Although they could not see everything in this one visit to the city, Rin made mental notes to how to reach the area on foot so she could come back. One of her biggest goals was to visit the art galleries. Kevin and Rin also talked about going to the movies, but there was just too much to do and see on this one day. They would make plans to see a movie later in the week, if possible. Kevin continued to hold Rin's hand or place his arms around her. He wanted to touch her and stay close to her throughout the day. He was clear about everyone knowing Rin belonged to him.

Rin and Kevin met another couple during that day's adventure. They were about ten years older than them. The couple was white, and Rin thought they seemed much older than their years.

"This must be the beautiful lady we heard about on the island," the woman said. Rin noticed she didn't say "black woman," and was pleased by that omission. She asked Rin and Kevin their names.

Kevin spoke up quickly and answered, "My name is Kevin, and this is my wife, Katherine." He introduced her as Katherine; no one called her Rin but him. "We are so happy to meet you," said Kevin. "What are your names?"

The man replied, "Our names are George and Phillis."

Rin thought they were a lovely couple but seemed curious about Kevin and herself. Kevin put it to rest when he said they were married. The couple seemed delighted to hear that. George commented on them being a handsome couple.

Phillis said, "You must have some beautiful children you're proud of."

Kevin went on to say they had been married for over twenty-five years and had two children and a couple of grandchildren. Rin noticed he enjoyed telling those lies; it made him happy, she thought. She watched his enjoyment as she nodded in approval.

It was apparent that the couple was very rich and had been on the island for a few months for a getaway. They apparently knew the island's owner. The couple enjoyed hearing Kevin's stories about their made-up family. They even invited Kevin and Rin's entire made-up family to one of their homes, a summer home in Vermont. In that moment, Rin thought Kevin was right to play married. It was fun and made things much easier when meeting people. He was displaying his love for her and fantasizing about the family they should have had together. It made him happy. It made Rin happy as well.

Kevin was keen to learn about the island. The development of land and the evolution of land always fascinated him. The island was formed about 1.5 million years ago by the volcano Palawai. The entire island is only 140 square miles in size. Southeast Lanai's Kaunolu Point is said to be the birthplace of the modern sport of cliff diving, begun by Hawaiian warriors leaping into the ocean from an eighty-foot ledge as proof of their courage. Rin looked at Kevin and asked if he was ready to jump from an eighty-foot ledge.

He said, "Anything for you, babe," and smiled. "But for sure, if you asked me twenty-five years ago, I would have definitely jumped off that ledge."

Rin knew the underlying meaning of what he said; if she had

given him the chance, they would have been married before she married Robert.

George laughed and said, "That's what I call love."

In 2012, Hawaii sold 98 percent of the island of Lanai to billionaire Larry Ellison. George explained there weren't any places in Lanai City that were too dangerous to visit. So those worries Kevin had earlier were not at all valid; he wanted to purchase those rings to show his love for Rin and to bring him closer to her. This validated Rin's first thought about playing married while on the island made Kevin very happy.

They even found out the only crimes on the island consisted of a fistfight at a bar and someone stealing mangos off a tree on private property.

Kevin said, "Who knew, babe? You can never be too careful."

The couple invited them to lunch, but Rin and Kevin politely declined; they wanted to have lunch alone. They found a quaint restaurant for a sandwich; Kevin had a beer, and Rin had water with lunch and then a glass of wine.

Chapter 25

Ordering in after a Long Day

Although they wore swimsuits underneath their clothes, they never got the chance to swim that day, but they did spend some time near the water. Rin removed her dress and got some sun. After being in the sun most of the day, her skin quickly went from medium caramel to a dark rich caramel color. When Kevin removed his shirt, Rin noticed how brown his skin had become as well, in that very short time. He often compared his arm to hers so she could see he was not far behind with his tan.

After walking for hours, they sat on the blanket Rin brought in her bag to rest for a while; the beach was a beautiful place to relax. As the sun began to set, they found their way back to the harbor to take the boat ride back to their villa. Rin asked Kevin if he wanted her to cook dinner. Kevin never learned to cook but would occasionally put a couple of steaks on the grill.

He said, "No, let's order in and take it easy. It's been a long, hot day."

Rin played some music and began to sing along as she undressed to shower before dinner arrived. If it was up to Kevin, he could listen to Rin sing all day. She was not a professional with a trained voice, but she still sounded wonderful. He wondered if she sang at her home for her family, because she seemed so happy when she sang. She never said so.

After undressing, Rin stepped into the shower and continued her singing, and of course Kevin joined her.

She reminded him, "Sweetheart, who's gonna answer the door when the food arrives?"

He said, "We got time; I need to get some of this sweat and sand off me too."

The shower was also big enough to sway to the music, so Rin continued to sing.

She said, "Well, join me then."

Rin thought she could get a quickie before dinner arrived. But that was not the case; someone was already knocking at the door before Kevin could remove his clothes.

Chapter 26

Making the Sweetest Love

Kevin answered the door and paid for the food and, as always, gave a generous tip. Sometimes, Rin thought his tips were too generous, but she was proud that he recognized the hard work of others. She got out of the shower and put her robe on; Kevin came back to shower and put on some shorts, no shirt. She reminded Kevin of her big terrycloth robe she wore when she sent him those nearly naked pictures last year, as well as that black sweater she had on with nothing underneath that showed a lot more than should be sent by text.

He said, "That's why I'm on this trip, babe; especially that black sweater."

They laughed. They ate dinner, Kevin drank a beer and Rin drank the wine they bought from the convenience store. By the time they went to bed, Rin had lost her desire for quickie. She wanted to spend some real time with Kevin as they lay together. She wanted to make love and explore every part of his body. She wanted every part of him.

Kevin noticed Rin was not as talkative that night, but she was in a very romantic and erotic mood, which really turned him on. But thought for a moment about how quickly this trip would go by; a discussion about their future together was imminent. He wondered what Rin was thinking about. He was hoping she was thinking the same about their future. But knowing Rin, she had some other complicated thoughts in that pretty head of hers as well.

They made the sweetest love that night. Kevin kissed every inch of her body. He kissed her in places that turned her on that she didn't even know existed. He used his tongue to caress places she never knew would turn her on.

She felt the same passion and said, "Sweetheart, what would you like me to do? Tell me what you want. Do you want something different? What can I do to make you feel as good as you make me feel? Please, let me make you happy. We've been apart for a long time, and I need to know if I can still satisfy you."

Kevin thought Rin was a natural at making him feel good; what could she be talking about? She massaged his back, his thighs, his neck, his butt, and at the same time used her tongue and sensual kisses to give him that tingly feeling all over his body. She caressed his breasts and played with his nipples with her fingers and lips. She made him wait a long time before going down on him; she was always amazed at how big he was, and she was never able to get all of him in her mouth.

The white boy with the big dick, Rin thought to herself. She spared nothing with what her hands could do for him down there. She then caressed his fingers with her tongue and kissed the tip of each one.

She said, "Sweetheart, please don't move, let me take care of you tonight. I got this. I promise."

She ended her caressing after a long time by going down on Kevin again. Taking it slow, using those techniques he used when he was inside her, that slow screw with her mouth, and using her hands in sync with her mouth to compensate for his size. She wanted them both to feel that out-of-body experience. She wanted him to feel like he was in a different world, on another planet, because that was how she felt. She stopped a moment to just look at him and smile. He was so turned on and seemed to be doing everything he could not to come before she placed him inside her. Rin was in charge, and she was driving him insane, but he continued to let her do it.

Rin knew Kevin was over-the-moon excited, so she whispered in his ear, "I won't let you come until you're inside me. I promise, baby. I know that is what you want. I want to eat you some more, so stop me when you're almost ready to come."

When the time came, Kevin stopped her. Then she straddled him on top and put him inside.

Kevin wanted desperately to put himself inside her or have Rin do it for him. He wanted to touch her and be a part of what she was doing to give her some pleasure as well, but she pushed his hands away. He grabbed her waist to help motion the rhythm.

She stopped him and whispered, "I got this, baby; be still. You relax and enjoy."

So she moved up and down slowly; she did circular motions and swayed from side to side. She wouldn't stop as he cried out. When he was about to come, he grabbed her waist to hold her down; she stopped moving so he could force himself to be all the way in when he came.

As always, Rin was wet and moist when loving Kevin. He always gave her multiple orgasms, so her satisfaction was intact. After making sure she satisfied him, she rolled off and snuggled up against him, with her butt up against his body, and went straight to sleep. She loved him so much but didn't want to say it right then. She just wanted him to feel the love she just gave him. She thought Kevin went to sleep as well, but she was too tired and too satisfied to find out.

Day 4.
Morning at
the Pool

Chapter 27

Kevin's Effect on Other Women

The next day, Kevin got up early and was ready to go for a swim in a pool near the villa. He didn't want to leave until Rin got up, but it wasn't long before she did. They kissed and said their good mornings. They had established a routine by then. He always headed out in the morning to swim and explore the island, purchase groceries or some items for Rin, or just take a walk. Rin didn't ask for a cleaning service; she preferred to clean the villa and do the washing herself; this gave her some alone time as well. Kevin pitched in sometimes with changing the bed and washing dishes. But Rin preferred that time by herself. Although she had a cleaning service at home, the leisurely time she had on the island, doing such housework gave her enjoyment, and she sang most of the time while doing it.

She always had breakfast prepared for Kevin when he returned from his morning outings. This was generally the only meal she cooked for the day. She was an okay cook, but it was not one of her passions in life.

That morning, Kevin was only gone for about fifteen minutes before he returned.

"Why are you back so soon?" she asked.

"I was just outside," he said. "I heard you sing and came back to listen. You know how I love to hear you sing, babe. You have a beautiful voice; it gives me a lot of joy. This is your calling."

"Beautiful to you only," she said, laughing. "I don't think so. It's strange, though; I haven't sung much until now. I sing when I'm happy."

That answered that question, and it made Kevin happy to hear it. He ate the light breakfast Rin prepared. She nibbled as she cooked, and then Kevin headed for the pool; he usually didn't eat much before a swim. Later that morning, Rin decided to join him at the pool, something she rarely did. She wanted to give him his morning space. But this morning, after their light breakfast, she packed a basket with snacks and champaign and orange juice to make mimosas at the pool.

She wore a one-piece dark green swimsuit that showed some cleavage, with a deep plunging back, with a multicolored sarong wrapped around her waist. Even in swimwear, Rin always dressed with class, elegance, and refinement. Her hair was swept up loosely at the top of her head, no makeup, but with large hoop earrings. As she neared the pool, she noticed several white women, some in their twenties, maybe thirties, watching Kevin swim. She recognized one of them from the restaurant that first day they arrived. She smiled to herself and thought, *So they found out his routine.*

Most of the women were probably there on vacation, girls' vacations or with their boyfriends or husbands, but they all look like tourists. Rin started to turn back but decided to keep going. As Kevin came out of the pool, she noticed how brown he had become. It was like watching a slow-motion movie of a gorgeous man coming out of the pool, glistening wet; it made you weak to look at him. Just then, a pretty young woman (with long blonde hair, of course) ran over to give him her towel. Kevin used the towel to dry off after motioning a thank-you to the young woman.

Rin stopped again; she wasn't jealous, but more self-conscious about being older, not as in shape as a younger woman and the contrast between them. She was also aware that she was the only woman of color at the pool. But she decided to stroll past Kevin and just take a seat by the pool. As she got closer, Kevin saw her, gave her a big smile, and waved. She waved back and headed to another chair. He came after her, grabbed her from behind, and then turned her toward him to give her a big kiss on the lips.

"Hey, babe," he said. "What did you bring in the basket?"

One could only imagine the look on the faces of those white women there. Their mouths swung open. *He's with her?* they must have thought. The ironic thing about the whole encounter is that Kevin didn't realize what was happening. He had no clue these women were even interested in him. He had no clue they were there just to look at that gorgeous man. And he had no clue how wonderful and special he made Rin feel at that moment. She thought, all Kevin saw at that pool was his Rin; he saw no one else. Kevin was enjoying his swim, but when he saw Rin walk toward him, as always, she took his breath away.

Chapter 28

A Day with Kai

Rin decided to join Kevin for a quick dip in the pool, and after spending some time there, she had some cordial conversations with the other women; actually, she had a good time. Kai happened to ride by on his bike as well; he stopped and gave Rin a kiss on the cheek.

Kai turned his head and saw Kevin and said, "Hey, Mr. Kevin."

Kevin smiled and said, "Hey, Kai."

Rin and Kevin were becoming part of that community. Neither of them sought this, but Rin admitted to herself it felt good just to be out in the open as a couple and for people to see them as a couple, as a family. She told Kevin that as well. However, that evening when they reflected on the afternoon, the discussion led to Rin reminding Kevin of their situation.

Rin told Kevin, "We're having an affair; it's still an affair, Kevin, even in this community."

Kevin responded, "Yes, it is, babe, but I've longed to let the world know how much I love you, how much I desire you as my wife, and it feels so good. And I have this chance, here and now. It's something I've dreamed about."

Rin had never heard him speak that way so clearly before. But why now? She loved him so much, and it frightened her. Kevin must know this was just a fantasy, and it would end soon.

They returned to the villa, showered together, and got dressed to begin their day in the Lania City. It was a wonderful and beautiful day to walk about the city. They ran into Kai and his mother. They were both so excited to see Kevin and Rin. Then Malia said she had to leave to go back to work.

Kai asked his mother if he could spend the rest of the day with Kevin and Rin.

Malia said, "That's fine, if it's okay with them," as she looked up at both of them for an acknowledgment.

Kevin said, "We'd be delighted to have Kai spend the day with us."

Rin smiled at them both and responded, "It would be my joy."

Kai ran to stand between them, took both their hands, and looked up, grinning from ear to ear. He was so proud to be with them.

They looked like a family, the most unusual family at that, Rin thought to herself. *Here we are, this white man from Finland, this beautiful Hawaiian boy, and then there's me. We must be something to look at.* But it brought her joy indeed.

That joy came because even though she didn't share Kevin's fantasy regarding their so-called marriage on the island, she really wished things could have been different. It was a mistake they didn't get together, a mistake they both paid for and tried desperately not to hurt anyone else because of it. To have a child with Kevin, to grow old together and have grandchildren, yes, spending time with Kai brought her joy in this way. To look at Kevin hold Kai's hand while she held the other put a smile on her face, but also brought sadness of what should have been.

They walked about, did some sightseeing, and shopped; Kevin asked Kai if he had eaten. He said, yes, but he could eat again. They sat outside of a quaint café and all ordered hamburgers and French fries because that's what Kai wanted to eat. Hamburgers and French fries weren't Rin's first choice; she rarely ate that kind of heavy food, but she wanted to order the same thing Kai ordered. She had grown very fond of him.

Kai asked a lot of questions as children do. He asked, "Do you have any children my age?"

Kevin said, "Well, we have a granddaughter almost your age." (Kevin was referring to his own granddaughter by his eldest son; she was about five. Of course, Rin knew all about her; Kevin had shared pictures. She was a beautiful child.)

Kai asked, "Is she pretty like Ms. Katie? Does she look like Ms. Katie? Is she nice like Ms. Katie?"

Kevin replied, "Of course she is; she's all those things. She's a very pretty little girl, and we're so proud of her."

Kai said, "When I grow up, I'm going to marry her. I want a wife that looks like Ms. Katie and is nice like Ms. Katie too."

Kevin smiled and whispered under his breath, where only Rin could hear him, "So do I, Kai; so do I."

As the afternoon turned into evening, Kevin said, "Well, Kai, it's getting late and time to go home. Your mother might be worried by now."

Chapter 29

Marilyn McCoo and Kevin Costner

After Kevin and Rin dropped Kai at home, they returned to their villa; when they went inside, they made love. Afterwards, Kevin said simply, "I love you, Rin. I really do."

She responded, "I love you too, sweetheart, with all my heart." As they lay in each other arms, Rin thought about something she wanted to ask Kevin all these years, so she just asked, "Before me, were you ever attracted to a black woman? I'm just curious."

He thought for a moment and commented, "Well, there was one I thought was very pretty. When I was in my teens, I had this big crush on Marilyn McCoo from the Fifth Dimension. I thought she was really something; I still do till this day. And no, Rin, you do not remind me of her; you're in a category all by yourself."

Rin laughed as she responded, "Of course I don't remind you of her. The old folks in my family would say, Marilyn McCoo is light bright, damn near white, and I'm not that. So Ms. McCoo doesn't count. Remember, I'm your caramel-colored babe."

Kevin smiled and asked, "So what about you? I know white men were not your thing back in the day. Did you have a crush?"

"You're right, I was not attracted to white men, and I'm still not attracted to white men, except for you, of course." She grinned. "But if I'm honest, I've always had a thing for Kevin Costner, but the chance of that happening is next to none. So I'm safe there."

Kevin commented, "Well, if that other Kevin had a chance to see you, I don't know, Rin; he may be laying here with you now."

Rin replied, "And if Marilyn got a chance to see you, she would have left Bill running."

They both had a good laugh and soon fell asleep.

Day 5.
Kevin's Changing Mood

Chapter 30

Kevin's Changing Mood

Kevin woke up before Rin, as usual. But this morning, he woke up much earlier and in a foul mood. He grew moody, sad, and intense as the morning went on. Rin had seen him that way before during their ten-year affair. She asked him what was wrong, but he didn't say. She went about preparing breakfast, washing clothes, and cleaning the villa, as was her usual routine. She noticed Kevin didn't go out for his normal morning excursion. She asked if he wanted to go out with her; she had some errands to run.

He grunted, "No," but said nothing more. So she left him alone and decided to go out on her own.

Rin was not the kind of woman to pester a guy until he explained himself, and she wasn't going to ask him if she did something wrong. Because all she did these last five days was to love him. So she ignored him, finished her chores, got dressed, and left. She was determined to enjoy this day on the island, even if it was without him. She might even see a movie. She probably needed some time alone as well, to help bring her mind out of this fog of a dream of being with Kevin. But before she left, she tried one more time to get him out of whatever funk he was in.

She said, "Goodbye, sweetheart. I'll be back in a couple of hours. Hopefully, you'll be in a better mood."

Rin knew it was the guilt of being there with her, leaving his wife and family, who depended on him for everything, but she didn't know what prompted it. Leaving his day-to-day life must have made him extremely guilty. She didn't feel that way about leaving her life behind for a few days. She needed this time with Kevin. But he seemed to be having second thoughts. It was Rin who planned the trip, anyway.

Before going down the road, she remembered the ring and doubled back to get it. She still hoped he would decide to join her, but he said nothing, so she grabbed the ring, placed it on her finger, and left for the day.

Chapter 31

The Argument

R in was gone for at least five hours before she noticed how late it was; it was close to dinner time. Even in his current mood, Kevin would still worry about her. But she wanted to make one more stop to visit the art gallery they passed by the other day; it looked amazing, and she really wanted to see the work inside. Art galleries did not interest Kevin, so this was a good time for her to spend some quality time there alone.

Rin went inside and met the gallery owner, Brad. They made a connection in their discussion about art; they were laughing and talking; she was impressed with his knowledge about art history. He invited her to an art show that was coming up.

Brad said, "This new up-and-coming artist will be showing some pieces here tomorrow night; he's wonderful."

Rin suspected Brad had a crush on this new artist; he looked cute in his picture. When she asked about the opening, Brad said it was a formal affair.

"Oh no," Rin said. "I have nothing to wear."

Brad responded, "Girl, have you been to this upscale boutique a few blocks away? There is this gorgeous orange dress that would look fabulous on you. Check it out."

Rin said, "I saw that dress a few days ago, and I really loved it, so beautiful and expensive too. But with my height and hips, I doubt if that store has anything that would fit me. It seems to cater to much smaller women."

"You're wrong, girl," Brad said as he handed Rin tickets to the opening. "Go check it out."

She thanked him with a big hug and turned to leave the gallery.

She looked up and saw Kevin coming through the door.

He looked angry; actually, he looked pissed off. But he tried to remain calm as he said forcefully, "Katherine, who was that guy? Your new boyfriend? And where have you been all day? I was worried."

Rin was mad that he called her "Katherine"; this conversation could soon escalate into a full-blown argument. "What the hell did you say to me?" she snapped.

Without waiting for his reply, she stormed out the door, and he followed. She thought about reminding him she was a grown woman who could take care of herself, but she didn't feel like making a scene. Kevin had already done that.

When they reached the sidewalk, she spun around and asked, "How the hell did you know where to find me, anyway? And that so-called guy you accused of being my boyfriend happens to be gay; Brad's the gallery owner."

"This is the second place I looked," Kevin said in an unsettling tone. "I knew you wanted to visit this art gallery, and you didn't think I wanted to because it's not my thing. So I figured I'd find you here. What are you trying to do, Rin? Do you want to punish me? I was very worried."

Rin gave him a pissed-off look, and they walked back in silence to the villa. He periodically told her she had been away so long and it scared him. He sounded apologetic when conveying his fears about Rin's long absence, but she thought he sounded ridiculous. And she was so mad at Kevin for causing that scene, she couldn't speak; it was best for her to say nothing. As they walked into the villa, Rin had calmed down a bit and told him she just wanted to give him the space he needed; she wasn't trying to punish him like he thought, and she surely wasn't meeting some random man.

But once inside the villa, as hard as she tried not to get angry, Rin let him have it: "Who do you think you are, Kevin? I can take care of myself. You were in a horrible mood this morning, and I was not going to sit around while you moped. I understand you feel guilty for being here with me; I really do, but if you didn't want to come, you should have stayed home."

She went to their room and closed the door but didn't slam it. She turned on the television set for company to calm herself down. She regretted saying he could have stayed home; neither one of them wanted that.

Chapter 32

Making Up

After a while, there was a knock on her door. And there was a man on other side, looking sheepish and beaten. That man was Kevin.

"Babe, I'm sorry," he said. "I don't know why I acted that way. You didn't deserve that."

Rin said, "It's about being guilty for being here with me, right?"

He said, "Yes, in part, but it's more than that. This trip will end next week, and I can't be without you anymore. I can't go back to the way it used to be with us. Not seeing each other, not being a part of each other's lives in the way we should be. I can't do it anymore, Rin. That caused my mood. I'm really sorry."

Rin said, "I understand, I really do, but it will be okay, sweetheart. We have no choice. Too many people depend on us. This is not about our lives. In this lifetime, our lives belong to others, but we'll be together forever in the next lifetime. We'll go back to the way it used to be with no problem, I promise, so let's enjoy the rest of the trip. The days are going by fast. And when we get home, we'll talk on the phone like we do and make sure everything is okay with each other. We'll continue to be each other's sounding board. Nothing will change from what it used to be."

Kevin said, "Babe, when you were gone for such a long time, in this place, where you know no one, I was really scared. I have always had this fear something will happen to you, and I won't be around to protect you, to help you. That fear was easier to deal with at home because I know you have people who love you and look out for you. And I do understand you can take care of yourself, but you are sometimes so unaware of your surroundings. You don't pay attention, and as I've always told you, not everyone is good."

She laughed and replied, "Sweetheart, I am a black woman with Persian blood running through my veins; who would be stupid enough to mess with me?"

Kevin smiled and just shook his head.

She noticed Kevin seemed exhausted. She motioned him to lay his head on her stomach and began to stroke his hair and caress his ears, lips, and neck ever so softly. She relaxed him until he fell asleep. They didn't make love that night, but she felt all the love she needed just watching him sleep and keeping him close. She smiled as she watched him breathe and fall into a deep sleep. She hoped he was having wonderful dreams that included her. She was happy and thankful to be with Kevin, but a sadness overwhelmed her as she continued to maintain the strength for her decision. She will help him to understand. However, she was going to make a lifetime of memories out of every moment on the island. The memories of the island would have to sustain them.

Day 6.
The Storm

Chapter 33

Kevin Washes Rin's Hair

The next morning, Kevin and Rin got up at the same time, very early. He apologized for his mood the prior day. And Rin apologized for her tone as well. They had had arguments before, so this was nothing new. But when you realize you have more years behind you than in front of you, it's terrifying when you yearn for the person you love.

They had planned to go out for breakfast that morning. Kevin wanted to give Rin a break from cooking. He heard her say she was going to wash her hair that morning as well. He wanted to do that for her and make up for his prior day's mood. It had been a sensual experience for both of them that first morning together.

Kevin took his time; he knew exactly what he was doing when it came to washing Rin's hair. While in the shower, he motioned her to face away from him but first took the opportunity to hug her close from the back and kiss her neck and shoulders, performing that grind she loved so much. He couldn't help touching her nipples and squeezing her breasts gently while the water ran on them.

He knew to comb her hair first to release any tangles. But he did so very slowly before taking the shower head to run warm water over it. He massaged her neck while the warm water ran over her body. He told Rin to lean her head back just a bit to angle more water around the edges of her forehead, while kissing the top of her forehead and kissing her neck. He went so far as to place his tongue gently in her ear, and she giggled. He noticed the deep dark waves the water made in her hair, as it fell down the middle of her back against her caramel-colored skin. Rin's skin color was absolutely beautiful to him; he had never seen anyone anywhere with that same coloring. She was so beautiful.

He began to soap her hair and to massage her scalp. The soap had now completely enveloped her hair, and he was careful not to get soap in her eyes.

He whispered, "Close your eyes, babe."

He began to perform slow circular massages as he felt her hair thicken at his fingertips. He also felt his fingertips tingle during the motions he made as well; it made him excited, and it was a special intimacy with Rin that he now enjoyed. Rin groaned and stepped back so their bodies touched.

He moved her away and said, "Not now, babe; later. Let me finish. He massaged the soap in her hair for a long while to give them both that tingly sensation they were experiencing a little longer.

He was already hard, and when Rin reached back to touch him, she sighed and said, "Skin over rock again, baby."

He said, "Not yet."

From Rin's moans and sensual movements, Kevin could see what she was experiencing equated to sensorial fireworks. He had never seen her so turned on. As he motioned her to lean her head backward, he applied the gentle pressure of warm water and the tender massaging touch of his fingers running through her hair in a froth of shampoo lather. Other than at the hair salon, no one had ever washed Rin's hair beside herself. The caring touch Kevin provided hit a trigger that connected to her desire for him.

Kevin began to rinse out the soap, and after the task was completed, he turned Rin to face him and put his arms around her to gently squeeze out the excess water in her hair. He pulled her hair down so she could look up and face him.

He gently kissed her lips for a long time and then said, "I love you, Rin. I love you with all my heart; you know that, right?"

She said, "Yes, I know that, baby. I know you love me. How could I not?"

Washing Rin's hair had become an erotic and intense sexual arousing that was new to them both. They then washed each other's bodies with more love than one can imagine. Every touch was fiery, passionate, and adoring. Even after all the lovemaking thus far during their stay on the island, it got better and better being together.

Chapter 34

The Intensity of Their Love

Kevin did not put himself inside Rin while in the shower, although she wanted him to. He said he had something else in mind. After they stepped out of the shower, he lifted her in his arms.

She said, "Baby, I'm too heavy, especially all wet."

Kevin said, "Babe, I have over fifty pounds on you; be quiet."

He lifted her effortlessly and carried her to bed; they were both dripping wet but didn't care. He gently laid her on her back and proceeded to open her legs ever so gently and placed his face in between them. He first began by licking her inner thighs and performing sweet kisses on her thighs and legs. He moved downward to kiss her feet and ankles and moved slowly back up to bury his head between her legs. He knew where her special spot was and used his tongue to satisfy her for a very long time; she felt overwhelmed. Those orgasms were nearly unbearable. She felt like she was in some alternative universe; this man knew how to show his love.

Rin knew he was hard as a rock by this time and needed her.

She motioned him upward, pulling on his arms so she could reach him to put him inside her. But he shooed her hands away like she had done to him a few nights before. Then he moved slowly up her body to kiss her navel and moved up toward her breasts (lingering for a time on her breasts until her nipples grew again as big as his thumb). He then lay down on top of her (their bodies still wet) to kiss her lips, lingering for a while, using his tongue to caress the outside of her lips as well as that sensual kiss with his tongue she was used to. She was turned on more and more each time he kissed her.

Then he kissed her cheeks and forehead, saying again, "Rin, I love you. Sometimes, I ache because I love you so much. I just ache for you, babe; I can't explain it."

Rin squirmed with delight and said, "Oh, my God, this man. Please, sweetheart, I need you. I need you inside me. Now! Right now."

Even still, he wasn't ready to do what she asked, what she begged.

He whispered, "In a minute, babe; you are so fiercely hot when I'm inside you. I'll come too quick. I'm too worked up right now; let me enjoy this beautiful body of yours."

He finally rose up to mount her, and there was no need for her to help him inside her. He was so hard, what he had to give her found its way inside Rin with no help at all. She smiled at him while she groaned and said, "There it is. Skin over rock, baby."

He went in and out slowly for as long as he could, and as always, Rin found his rhythm. When he sped up to come, they came together, but Rin had had many orgasms before that.

Rin thought that was the most beautiful morning of lovemaking she had ever experienced with Kevin, and that was saying a lot. They lay there a minute to catch their breath, not saying a word.

Finally, Rin said, "I love you so very much. I always have and

I always will, no matter what happens. Always remember that, sweetheart. Promise me you'll remember?" Rin hoped Kevin didn't sense the desperation in her voice as he nodded and smiled.

Kevin grabbed her gently and whispered, "I can't remember what my life was like without you in my heart, and I never want to. You are an amazing woman, babe."

Then he got up to get a warm wet towel to wash Rin and himself down there. They didn't have time for another shower.

"What a mess you made," he said, laughing.

He made a big grin when Rin accused him of making the mess and said it was mostly his doing. He had to admit that when he came this time, he kept coming. After he finished the cleanup and kissed her down there, they got dressed, headed out to find breakfast somewhere, and began a day of exploring the uncommercialized areas of the island.

Chapter 35

The Boho Bag

At this point, many of the islanders and some of the tourists had come to know Kevin and Rin. So when they found a small, quaint breakfast place, it wasn't a surprise they knew a few of the folks, including both the patrons and workers. Kevin asked about a good walking path to explore and got directions to an area of interest. Upon approaching the pathway, Rin was amazed at the beauty it displayed; the trees, flowers, and birds were both exquisite and wonderful, something to remember. It was warm and sunny when they started out. They both wore gym shoes for walking, tank tops, and long shorts; they wanted to be comfortable.

Before they left for breakfast, Rin packed her usual boho bag to take with them. Kevin complained about how much stuff she brought along. He also complained because Rin packed so much stuff, and it got too heavy for her to carry around all day, so he had to hold it for her. He thought the bags were too feminine for him. But he carried them anyway.

This morning, Rin grabbed her most colorful cross-shoulder

bag with its rainbow of colors, just to make him cringe; she loved this bag the most. And she knew Kevin especially hated this one. She added water, snacks, a blanket, and a light rain jacket for both of them, just in case, even though it was a gorgeous day and there was no sign of rain.

They were going to explore the uncommercial areas of the island, so Rin packed everything they might need. The bag wasn't heavy at all, so she swung it around her neck in the cross-body format and was ready to go. She had not planned to shop that day, so she decided to add two more bottles of water. Before they left, Kevin decided to take a cigar with him; he wanted to try the one that was recommended at a smoke shop he visited. He didn't want to smoke it at the villa, although he knew Rin wouldn't mind. He threw the cigar and lighter in Rin's bag as well. She looked at him cross-eyed, stuck out her tongue, and laughed.

"So the bag is good enough for that stinky cigar, huh?" She laughed louder.

Chapter 36

Exploring the Island, the Storm begins

Their outing was an old-fashioned extraordinary nature walk. It was an opportunity to relax, take their time, and explore the beautiful environment they were in. They enjoyed the breathtaking sights of pineapple farms. Lanai is often referred to as "Pineapple Island" because of its agricultural history. It is the sixth largest of the Hawaiian Islands, although Kevin and Rin could not possible explore the entire 140 square miles on foot, the path allowed them to see much of it from afar. They could view its extremely diverse landscape, offering everything from arid desert to snowcapped mountains. There are rivers, streams, waterfalls, vertical cliffs, extinct tuff cone volcanoes, tranquil bays, and high-elevation plateaus. The folks who lived there told them the term *Lanai* is Hawaiian for a porch or a veranda, in a tropical-type climate. Lanai was all so beautiful; they were unplugged from the world and loved every minute of it.

After they had hiked for nearly three hours, they decided to take a rest and then head back. Kevin was hungry, and he was sure Rin was hungry as well. Those few snacks she packed were not enough for a decent lunch. He also noticed a few raindrops as he looked up at the sky. It was still sunny, but he had a feeling it was going to become cloudy soon, and more consistent raindrops were sure to follow. Kevin was used to working outside as a developer and was able to gauge weather changes very effectively.

He turned to Rin and said, "Babe, we have to head back; it's going to pour down rain soon, I'm sure."

Rin began to feel the raindrops as well, so she immediately pulled out the rain gear from her bag. The wind was starting to blow a little harder, and it was difficult to put them on.

Rin laughed as she said, "Aren't you glad I brought this?"

Rin noticed that although Kevin smiled, he had this worried look on his face. He kept looking up at the skies and the path before them leading back.

Kevin had secured his raingear on his body tightly first, and then he proceeded to help Rin. Just like the instructions on an airplane: Make sure the mask is in place for yourself first before you proceed to help someone else.

But by the time he started to help Rin, the winds became violent, and branches were falling everywhere. Her face was wet, and neither of them could see very well because it began to pour.

He smiled at her so she wouldn't worry and said, "Your hair is blowing everywhere, Rin. I'm not washing it tonight. And how am I supposed to get all this hair underneath the hood of this raincoat?"

She smiled. He grabbed her bag and placed it under his raingear and made sure that Rin was protected as much as he could with hers. He grabbed her by the hand tightly, and they began hiking back.

They only got a few yards when the gusty winds became excruciatingly violent, and the cloudbursts sounded like cannons.

The rain felt like buckets of water being thrown at them as they walked against the wind. Heavy branches were falling from the trees, and it was unsafe for them to be in the open; the trail was no longer safe. They had to find shelter. He remembered a small cabin about a quarter-mile back, and they headed that way. It was extremely difficult to see, walk, and dodge falling debris, but Kevin held Rin's hand tight, pulling her along.

Chapter 37

Storm becomes Violent; Finding Safety

While struggling through the rain and wind, and holding tightly to Rin's hand, Kevin heard a loud crack and looked up to see a large tree branch falling toward them; it had broken off from this humongous tree. He let go of Rin's hand and pushed her backward hard as he stepped back at the same time. The large branch fell between them; it was at least thirty inches in diameter and could have killed them surely. Kevin called out for Rin but couldn't see her or hear her respond as he began to climb over the branch.

He shouted louder, "Rin!"

He was scared and terrified. He continued his climb and saw where Rin had fallen backward, away from the tree, thank God.

"Rin," he shouted. "Are you okay?"

She couldn't speak at first but began to sit up. He jumped toward her and repeated, "Babe, are you okay? Are you okay?"

Rin said, "Yes, I'm fine. I just need a minute."

Kevin said, "Are you hurt? Can you walk?"

Rin said, "I'm fine. Really, I'm fine, sweetheart. But why did you push me?"

Kevin just shook his head and thought, *Same old Rin; never seems to notice what was happening around her.*

He helped her up from the ground, and she climbed over the tree branch. He told her they must keep moving quickly and to keep holding his hand. He made that split-second decision to let go only to keep her safe. Each step was brutal as they walked against the wind, and the rain kept coming down in buckets.

They soon reached the small cabin, or better described as a shack. Kevin wanted to inspect its safety first; he wanted to make sure the foundation and floors were solid and the walls, beams, columns, and roof were secure. His career as a builder/developer came in handy at that very moment. After the inspection, surprisingly so, he decided it was still structurally sound, but there were no windows or doors, which made them realize no one lived there.

Kevin had positioned Rin near the cabin, away from the rain and high winds, until the inspection was over. He went back to get her, and they went into the cabin. It was very small (maybe fifteen by fifteen feet at the most), but at one time, it must have been beautiful. The winds began to die down, and the temperature was warm, but the rain just kept coming. With the winds no longer an issue, there was no need to secure the door and window; they were small entryways, anyway.

Kevin said, "The cabin was originally built solid to have held up all this time, although there's really no way to tell how long it's been here."

"Who cares?" said Rin. "It's perfect."

There was a fireplace. Kevin inspected that as well to ensure the chimney would allow for at least a small fire.

"It's all good, Rin; we can build a fire. There's plenty of wood in this cabin we can use, and it's pretty dry."

She quipped, "And what will you use to start the fire, sweetheart? We don't have any matches."

"Babe, remember that lighter I put in your bag for my cigar? Thank God for that bag you brought; I'll never complain again about carrying those ridiculous bags of yours. I promise, babe. I really, really promise."

Even with the raingear, they were both soaking wet, but the contents in Rin's boho bag were still pretty dry. Kevin kept it close under the rain gear while carrying it.

Chapter 38

The Cabin

It took a minute, but Kevin finally started the fire. He had them take off their wet clothes and lay them next to the fire to dry out. They kept on their underwear. He then wrapped the blanket around them and suggested they drink one bottle of water each, saving the snacks for breakfast, just in case they had to wait out the storm and walk home the next morning. It was at least a five-mile walk back, and they would need the energy. They each would have another bottle of water as well. But Kevin only took a few swallows from his water bottle. He saved the rest in case Rin needed extra. He thought again about how smart Rin was, always prepared. She prepared them both for what might happen. He loved her so much.

In that same moment, Rin thought about how Kevin was naturally and instinctively protective her; she was always first. He may complain about something as silly as a boho bag, but nothing was more important than her safety. She was grateful for his instincts and his natural ability to observe his surroundings. He was an amazing man, and she was so grateful for the kind of man he was. She loved him with all her heart.

Rin was not afraid at all. She was there with Kevin. So they spent about an hour just talking about the day and the beauty of the island, discussing the day's events and the struggle to get to that shack. She listened as he when on about the land being a developer's dream, and how he expressed a little anger about someone changing it and how they would have to come through him first. He was grateful for the billionaire who owned it and his commitment to keep the land's beauty intact.

Kevin's mood then changed again, to a kind of familiar sadness.

Rin asked, "Are you thinking about your family? It would stand to reason after what just happened. It's okay, baby."

"No, Rin, I'm not thinking about my family. I'm thinking about you. What if something happened to you today? I couldn't bear it. I'm always afraid I'll lose you."

Rin gently reminded Kevin that she was not his to lose. She tried to lighten the mood with a laugh, saying, "Kevin, remember, I'm the other woman."

He frowned at her and said, "Rin, you are my woman, and you know what I mean; you're too much. I just can't lose you."

Rin said, "Kevin, I love you; I always will. That's enough, baby; it's enough until the next lifetime. Remember? We've talked about this many times.

She went on to say she was never jealous about the life he had with Sarah. She was happy he had someone who cared for him and loved him. She understood there was love and sex in his life these past fifteen years, and he absolutely needed that kind of emotional and physical connection. She didn't mind at all. She wanted his life to be happy and full. She also understood his responsibilities to his family, and she would play no part in destroying it. She knew if Kevin ever left, it would be devastating to Sarah; she couldn't survive without him. She was totally dependent on Kevin, financially and emotionally. There were also the children, although the oldest two were grown, with Brian, the oldest, now married with a little girl; the youngest was still in high school. She knew his family needed him very much. Kevin's leaving would destroy a lot of people, and she would not allow it. As she spoke, Kevin put his face in his hands, nearly in tears.

Kevin told Rin his financial success was because of her. She provided him with legal advice, and she was his sounding board on every major decision. She performed research and made sure her legal teams were on top of every move he made. She was the smartest person he knew. And although they did not see each other for fifteen years, she was his partner, she was his rock, and everything he had was because of her.

She told him, "Sweetheart, do you know how many clients you referred to me that resulted in millions for my law firm? You may not realize how much you've done for me. Where many businesses would not take a chance on a small law firm run by a black woman, you opened those doors for me. My success and wealth are because of you as well."

This was the first time they acknowledged this to each other. They fought for each other's business successes as much as they fought for their own. They did what they did because they loved each other, and as a result, that love led to their success and wealth.

Rin knew Kevin had her heart. And she had his. Throughout their twenty-five years, he was the first person she wanted to tell when things went wrong and when they went right. But she had some secrets. There were still some things she needed to tell him, some important things. He was the light in her life, and knowing him was the best thing that had ever happened to her. Nothing said or done can be regretted in that regard.

Chapter 39

What about this Lifetime

But even with all those feelings for Kevin, God came first in her life, then her daughter Blu, and then Kevin. She was a survivor in every sense. She was, indeed, independent, but she would forever ache for Kevin; that would not change. She absolutely knew what Kevin meant about that ache he had. She had it too. On the other hand, she also understood how Kevin felt about her relationship with Robert. Kevin wanted there to be someone to watch out for her and keep her safe, so to speak. Even though she was very independent, she had to acknowledge she could sometimes be unaware of her surroundings.

She also knew it gave Kevin comfort there was someone in her life who cared for her. But she also knew he hated the thought of her making love to another man, even Robert, especially Robert; it bothered him tremendously. But that was out of his control. If it was up to him, she would not have slept with anyone but him, no matter the length of time in between.

Kevin never understood Rin's philosophy of the "next lifetime." It was this lifetime he was thinking of. He wanted her now, in this life, more than ever. He just didn't know how to make that happen, but he'd find a way. He loved his sons, and he cared for Sarah; the life they had together was satisfactory. However, Rin was his everything; it was Rin he loved.

Their clothes were dry within the hour, so they put them back on and soon fell asleep in each other's arms, wrapped in the blanket. The night was warm and pleasant. There were a few insects to contend with, but nothing severe. Nevertheless, Kevin slept lightly; he watched Rin carefully, as he was concerned she may have been hurt from the fall; she may have hit her head, but he didn't find any sign of a bump upon his inspection.

Day 7.
After the Storm

Chapter 40

Getting Ready for a Fight

After staying up most of the night watching Rin sleep and making sure they were safe, Kevin fell asleep. He didn't mean to. He started to wake Rin before he closed his eyes so they could start the journey back but decided against hiking in the dark. They would, indeed, wait until the morning light.

Kevin woke when he heard a growling sound and jumped up, fearing an animal had entered the cabin. With the sunlight in his eyes, Kevin couldn't tell what kind of animal it was or how large it might be. He only heard a sinister growl. Rin awakened and shouted for Kevin; he shushed her to be quiet. He knew she was frightened. But Rin slowly came to her feet and stood beside him. He quickly shoved her behind him without taking his eyes off the animal in front of them. Rin slowly kneeled to pick up a big stick and moved again to stand beside Kevin. But Kevin shoved her behind him again, glancing at her with an angry look.

Fortunately, it was a search dog; the villagers had been worried about them. Kevin and Rin were known throughout the island community; folks liked the couple a lot. One of the neighbors alerted public safety of their excursion and said they must have been caught in the storm. They checked their villa, and they had not returned. So as soon as the morning light came, they began a search.

They both were very happy to see the police rescue team so they wouldn't have to find their way back on their own. The team led them to their vehicle and drove them back to their villa. After arriving home, they showered, climbed into bed, and slept most of the day.

They arose from their nap and ordered take-in because there was no way they felt like leaving the villa that night. They had begun to like traditional Hawaiian food and ordered chicken laulau with some side dishes to go with their beer and wine. Kevin watched Rin walk around the villa, just talking to herself about something. He watched her but paid no attention to what she said. He gave one-word answers like he was listening to her. She had on a T-shirt, and her hair was piled on top of her head, falling periodically in her eyes. She looked so cute to him, he just wanted to watch her.

Kevin said to himself, "Rin is okay. My Rin is safe."

It could have been different. There was debris falling everywhere, and she could have been hurt. He couldn't stand for her being hurt.

Kevin said, "Babe, please stop talking; just relax, and come sit by me."

He put on an old movie to watch while they waited for dinner. Rin sat near him on the couch and put her feet and legs in his lap.

He asked her, "Why didn't you stay behind me when the dog came into the shack? I didn't want you to get hurt."

She said, "I didn't want you hurt either, for God's sake. We fight together like we always have; this may have not been business, but it was still our fight together. Your instinct is to always protect me, but I'll never let you be hurt, either, if I can help it. What I do and the decisions I make are for you too, sweetheart."

Within Rin's mind, keeping Kevin from being hurt was also keeping them apart. It was the right thing to do, no matter how much they loved each other. There was so much more to consider than their love for each other right now.

Chapter 41

Kevin Got Jokes

Kevin knew what she said dealt with more than what happened after the storm but didn't want to delve any deeper at that moment. He knew they still had time to discuss things, and there was so much more he wanted to tell her. He wanted to make plans to be together. They would have that discussion soon, long before the end of their vacation. So he just smiled and began to inspect her legs for insect bites and bruises from the fall as well as her arms, neck, and head. She had some, but nothing to be concerned about. And most important, there were no bumps on that beautiful head of hers. Kevin began to caress her legs and move his hands upward between her thighs because he knew she wore nothing under her T-shirt.

"Sorry, Rin," he said, with a sheepish grin. "Just checking for more bruises and bites."

She said, "Sweetheart, don't start something you can't finish; dinner will be here soon."

Kevin said, "We have time for a quickie, don't you think?"

Rin felt him, and he was indeed hard already, with no effort from her. "Where did this come from?" she asked.

She unzipped his pants, wrapped her legs around him while facing him, and proceeded to slide him right in her. Just when they were getting heated, the doorbell rang. Rin groaned and jumped up to pay for the food.

Kevin said, "Damn, Rin, I just needed one more second."

When she returned with their dinner, Kevin said, "Baby, come back here."

She replied, "I would think the doorbell ring would have calmed that thing down."

He caressed himself and stroked himself in front of her (Rin admired how hard he still was; it stood straight up).

Kevin said, "See, babe, I've been keeping it up for you. Please come back; it won't take long."

Rin replied, "This better be quick, Kevin; I'm really hungry. We haven't had much to eat these past twenty-four hours."

She walked toward him, removing her T-shirt; she was completely naked.

She quickly mounted Kevin as he sat on the couch. He wasn't wearing a shirt, just those unzipped pants. So her breasts were pressed up against his chest as she thrashed about on top of him, side to side, up and down, fast and slow. There was no kissing, just lust. It felt amazing to them both, really good, hot as always. They were laughing and having fun. Rin stayed wet even thinking about having sex with Kevin.

When he finally came, he patted her bottom, motioning for her to get off him, and said, "Let's eat, babe."

Rin said, "That was a long fuck. I thought this was supposed to be a quickie."

Kevin responded, "I wanted to give you time for some satisfaction as well. In the words of Bernie Mac, 'I got mine; I hope you got yours.'"

"Oh, you got jokes," Rin said and then smacked him on the back of the head.

They laughed as they ate, staying away from any talks about what their future would look like together. Rin wanted to wait until the end of the trip to try to explain everything. There was so much to tell Kevin. And he didn't even know how to begin the conversation just yet. He knew she may not want to leave Robert, out of loyalty. How could he ask her to do that?

The television was on. They watched *Witness for the Prosecution*, an old Tyrone Power movie made in 1953. It was one of Rin's favorites; Kevin knew that. However, if he had a choice for an old movie by Tyrone Power, it would have been *The Mark of Zorro*, released in 1940.

As they got ready for bed, Rin's thoughts drifted, and she quietly thought of the future plans she had for her own life, a life without Kevin. At the same time, she just couldn't imagine something happening to him. She believed that if something happened to him, she would just die. He always talked about her safety and her well-being. The truth was, her connection to him was something she couldn't even describe to herself. But she knew she could not be on this earth without him on it too. As long as Kevin was okay, whether she was with him or not, she could go on living. After dinner, they fell asleep in each other's arms on the couch before the movie ended. About midnight, Kevin carried Rin to bed as she laid her head on his shoulder; they both slept soundly and didn't wake up until the next morning.

Day 8.
The Art Gallery

Chapter 42

Kevin's Wife

Kevin thought about that terrible mood he was in a few days ago, resulting from a phone call from his wife. He took it out on Rin, and that was wrong. He didn't tell Rin about the call, but it surely ruined that day. It was not unusual for Sarah to be upset about the times he had to be away from home for business trips. She just could not make decisions without him and would make all kinds of excuses for him to come home. But this particular call affected him because he was with Rin, and there was a lot of guilt regarding that. Was the guilt because he was cheating on his wife? Or was the guilt because she interrupted the precious time he was having with the woman he desperately loved? What kind of man was he? Decisions had to be made. He couldn't continue to live this way.

He had not been with Rin for a long time, and he needed this; he needed to be with her. He felt terrible about it and struggled with the commitment he made to his wife and the undeniable ache he had for Rin. He realized the pain he felt for this transgression was not all about Sarah, but about the limited time he had with Rin. Again, what kind of person was he?

Kevin knew Sarah cared for him and appreciated the good home she helped to provide him and their three boys. Rin was the only other woman in his life during their entire marriage. But that surely didn't make it right. He still cheated on his wife. But he was not in love with Sarah, not the way he should have been.

Kevin put his head into his hands and said softly, "God, please help me. I'm not a bad man."

Rin was who he wanted. It was always Rin. How could he have taken all that out on her? She was right; all she had ever done was to love him, to put him first in the best way she knew how, under any circumstance. And at the same time, Kevin wondered about Robert. He just realized Rin hadn't mentioned him once during this trip. What were her feelings for him now? He hated to ask himself this question again, but he wondered if Rin would leave her husband for him.

With everything between them and with everything that kept them apart, after all these years, Kevin was more in love with Rin than ever. He had a strong, almost inexplicable desire for her. The excitement and wonder of early love, of mutual discovery, of delighting in fantasies, and anticipating any possibility of sharing a life with her, was as new as it was twenty-five years ago. He still ached for Rin; he yearned for her. He thought of Rin every day (sometimes all day) and craved this opportunity to finally spend time with her again.

Chapter 43

The Orange Gown and Silver Bow Tie

After he acted like a fool, Kevin decided to make it up to Rin by taking her to the art gallery's opening. He saw the information the gallery owner gave Rin the day of their argument. It was a formal affair, and neither of them had anything to wear that was elegant enough to attend. So during his morning excursion, he went to the shop that displayed a dress Rin had admired earlier in the week; it was bright orange with the silver sequins. It was indeed beautiful, and Rin would be gorgeous in it. He knew she was taller than most women, and she was stacked, as they say, but he couldn't remember what size she wore. Unfortunately, that dress was the only one, and he hoped it would fit. He thought, *Look at me, in a dress shop buying a dress for my woman*. He had to laugh. He had never done that before and was a little embarrassed.

Kevin told the saleslady he would take the dress and to wrap it up in a beautiful box.

She said, "That will be $11,039.27."

He knew it was expensive, but he wanted Rin to have it. So he bought the dress, along with a silver bow tie for himself to match the silver embellishments of the dress; the saleslady recommended it. Luckily, he brought a black suit and white shirt with him on the trip. He also remembered the silver pumps Rin wore that first night they were together; they would go perfectly with the dress. He laughed at himself again. It wasn't like him to think about accessories like silver bow ties and silver pumps. What a woman wears and with whatever kind of accessories never mattered to him. But it was Rin he was thinking about. He thought back to the first day he saw her in that office building. He remembered that off-white linen suit she wore, with the pencil skirt that hit just above her knee, and that black tank top underneath her jacket. And those high-heel black pumps on those beautiful bare caramel-colored legs. He even recalled the hooped earrings that she still wears today. She was always put together so beautifully. He recalled that first day he saw her often; it was forever etched in his mind.

Chapter 44

Will the Orange Gown Fit?

After returning from the boutique, Kevin waited to tell Rin they would be going to the opening; he knew that would make her very happy, and he wanted to wait as long as possible to spring the surprise. She loved the art world. Although he didn't care much for that kind of thing, he recalled how she explained that art helps you process your emotions and understand the beauty of your surroundings. This was funny to Kevin; Rin never paid much attention to her surroundings regarding her safety, but she was quick to pick out the landscape beauty of this world. She also taught him art allows you to see life from a different perspective and makes you feel alive. She told him art was also part of his world in the commercial development arena, and whether he knew it or not, it was a tool for cultural exchange, education, and expression. Kevin was now looking forward to the show as well because he saw the possibilities through Rin's eyes and her heart.

He hated to compare Rin to Sarah, but she was an exciting woman. Just speaking with her on the phone these past fifteen years brought meaning, thrills, exhilaration, and sensations to his life.

She stimulated his soul and his spirit. She made him look forward to each day. She was electrifying.

Later that afternoon, when Rin asked where they would be having dinner, Kevin gave her the dress box and told her they would be going to the gallery opening. And he apologized once again for putting her through it that day he found her there.

Rin was ecstatic and overwhelmed. She loved art, especially attending grand art shows. This made her very, very happy. She threw her arms around him and gave him a big kiss on the cheek. The fact that he would be taking her made it all so sweet. She knew he was not interested in this kind of thing, but he went through all this trouble for her.

"Thank you, baby," she said. "Thank you so much. I didn't think you wanted to go. Especially since we had that big argument that day. You are so sweet. I love you."

Kevin was excited as he watched Rin remove the dress from the box. She was overjoyed to see it was the orange and silver dress she admired in the window. She told him how beautiful the dress was but complained it was too expensive, all while having a big smile on her face. However, when she removed the dress from the box and checked the size, she looked concerned.

Kevin said, "What's wrong, babe? I thought you loved this dress."

Trying not to hurt his feelings, she said, "Baby, I'm not sure if this dress will fit. It's a size 6, and I probably need a size 8 or maybe a size 10. And you know how tall I am." But she reassured him, "I'm sure it will fit, baby; don't you worry, I'll make it fit. I brought a full-body foundation garments with me. I didn't think I would need it, but it might help. Let me shower, do my hair, and put on my makeup first. This may take an act of God, and we'll need to be ready to roll, if we can get it zipped."

She knew the dress cost at least ten grand. But he still had that terrified look on his face.

"Don't worry, baby," she assured him.

Kevin took a long look at Rin's body and noticed she had lost some weight. She never ate much anyway when the weather was warm, and with all the walking exercise and sex activity, she did look like she lost some weight. He meant to mention it before, that maybe she wasn't eating enough; he liked her the size she was. Maybe it was all wishful thinking; he did enjoy Rin's size in every way possible. She was very curvy, she was stacked, but if weight loss helped her get into this dress tonight, she could gain all the weight back tomorrow and then some, for all he cared. He just wanted to take her to the art gallery tonight.

After Rin showered and did her makeup, she pulled a black foundation garment from her suitcase. She stepped into it, and while Kevin pulled it up from the back, she tugged on it from the front.

He said, "Baby, I don't know; you got this beautiful butt and all this cleavage. I don't think we'll be able to bring this thing up over all this. I don't think we're going to get this on you."

She said, "Start from the bottom, sweetheart, and keep tugging."

They both pulled and tugged, and started to laugh at the same time until they lost their balance and fell on the bed. Rin laughed so hard she ruined her makeup and had to retouch it.

They finally got it on her, and Kevin asked, "How do you plan to use the bathroom? You won't be able to have a drink or even drink water."

She laughed again, pulled at the crotch of the garment, and said, "See this hole? It makes a way for me to pee, and to do other things, don't you think?"

Kevin inspected the hole himself with his finger and looked

up at her with that grin. "Well, I got plans for this when we return. Let's not take it off right away, babe."

After she repaired her makeup, she stepped into the gown, and Kevin was able to zip it up effortlessly. The gown had spaghetti straps and a plunging neckline, trimmed in silver rhinestones. She removed from her bag a diamond pendant with a delicate silver chain that Kevin had bought her many years ago. He remembered it immediately, as it brought brief sadness to him. He had exchanged that necklace for the engagement ring he originally bought her those many years ago, but he smiled that it had great meaning to her. After he ensured it was safely around her neck, he released the clamp in her hair to let it fall around her shoulders and back. Her hair gleamed in shining coal-black spirals and cascaded everywhere.

Rin turned around as he stepped back to admire how beautiful she was. She then sat on the bed to place the silver pumps on her feet.

He knelt beside her and said, "Let me, my beautiful queen; you look like you should be in a fairy tale book."

She remembered that first day in the villa when she saw Kevin and that silly thought about him looking like a king in a fairy tale. They were both so silly. As he placed those pumps on Rin's feet, Kevin recalled that first night they were together when Rin wore that baby blue nightie and those same silver pumps. He rose from where he knelt and took Rin's hands to help her from the bed. They stood together, nearly eye to eye, shoulder to shoulder because of those five-inch heels.

Kevin reminded himself to breathe and then said, "Rin, you look gorgeous; the dress fits your body perfectly. Every curve is accented just perfectly. As I've said to myself many times, Mother Nature and God himself spent a lot of time on you, babe; you are gorgeous."

Rin asked, "You think it looks okay? Is it too tight?"

Kevin said, "Absolutely not; it's perfect. You're perfect."

Chapter 45

Kevin Believes in a Higher Power

Because of Rin, God became more important to him throughout these past twenty-five years. He always believed in a higher power. However, because of Rin, he believed in God and his power more and more each day. Kevin wondered if God made Rin just for him. Was Rin his gift from God? She had been a constant in his life; she was everything good in his life. Kevin knew this sounded nuts because they did not have a life together, like they should have. And they had sinned in God's eyes for a long time. But God had to know the wrong choices they made to not be together, with all signs indicating they should have been together all those years ago, those wrong choices were not of God's doing. It was of their own doing, and for all the wrong reasons. God would have to forgive them. He gave them many opportunities to marry and be together openly; they were just stupid. God would forgive stupid.

Kevin shivered a second to bring himself out of his gaze at Rin and his thoughts of the past. "So how do I look, babe?"

Rin said, "My goodness, sweetheart, I was so worried about this dress, I didn't even see how handsome you are."

Kevin wore a black suit, white shirt, and silver bow tie. He would only wear silver for her, and she knew it. It made her smile.

"You are, indeed, the most handsome man I know. Just ask any woman on this island, they will tell you the same. And by the way, I absolutely love that silver bow tie."

He kissed her cheek and said, "Thank you, sweetheart. Thank you with all my heart; you're beautiful too."

Chapter 46

Enjoyment at the Art Gallery

They took a cab to the gallery, and when they arrived, it was clear they were the most stunning couple there. Everyone wanted to meet them and learn more about them. The art exhibition was wonderful; it was everything Rin thought it would be. She and Kevin spoke with Brad and thanked him for the tickets, and Kevin apologized for his behavior at the gallery.

Brad said, "No problem; if I had her hips, I would hope my man would be worried about me as well." Brad also admired how beautiful Rin looked in that dress. "I told you it would fit, girl."

They all laughed.

Many up-and-coming artists exhibited their work, but a new artist was all the rage. His work provided a window to the past of the art world and at the same time glimpses of the future.

Rin told Kevin, "It's always interesting to see what is going on in the world of fine arts. New trends develop over time, while others fade away into history books. Visiting an art gallery enhances simple brain functions and awakens your visual imagination."

Rin was beaming and hoped Kevin got a better insight into her enjoyment; he was so sweet to be a part of this experience with her and listen as she went on and on about something she was sure was relatively boring to him.

But Kevin enjoyed it as well; he really did. He joked, "The top-shelf drinks and hors d'oeuvre that were served helped me enjoy myself quite a lot."

She just rolled her eyes at Kevin and then smiled.

Kevin and Rin spoke with some of the artists. Kevin asked Rin if she wanted him to purchase a piece for her. She said she wanted to wait and think about it. But he noticed which pieces interested her most and planned to make a purchase after the show.

During the evening, Kevin proudly introduced Rin as his wife, Katherine; it gave him comfort and happiness. It was an enchanting evening for them both, like a fairy tale. They held hands most of the time and were never physically apart for long that evening.

Chapter 47

Rin's Divorce

As they were saying their goodbyes and getting ready to leave, they both heard a woman's voice call out, "Katie, is that you?"

Kevin and Rin looked at each other, startled, and turned to see who it was. It was an old friend of Rin's; her name was Chioma. Chioma was Nigerian but was raised in London and came from a boat load of money. Her family was one of Rin's important clients, and they became good friends over the years.

After they embraced, Chioma said, "Oh my goodness, Kate, I'm so glad to see you; it's been a long while. How are you?" But before Rin could answer, Chioma said, "I heard about your divorce. I'm so sorry; it's been about three years, right? Are you okay? You look fabulous, girl. I tried to get in touch with you, but you seemed to have fallen off the face of the earth. Robert was a good guy, but we all wanted you to be happy, girl."

Kevin tightened his grip on Rin's hand in absolute surprise, trying not to say anything. His grip was so tight, he hurt her fingers. She glanced at Kevin, trying not to show any emotion, and motioned him to release his grip on her hands just a bit, as she wiggled her fingers. She could see the hurt and anger in those blue eyes. She could always tell how Kevin felt by those blue eyes.

She told Chioma, "Yes, I'm doing well, and I'm so sorry for not returning your calls and reaching out. It was just something I had to deal with alone. You look wonderful too, girl. So good to see you. But let me introduce you to my new husband, Kevin. We got married shortly before coming to the island. This is our honeymoon. It was sudden, and we haven't had time to make any formal announcements yet." She thought that would help calm Kevin just a bit.

Chioma said, "I'm so glad to meet you, Kevin. Wow, Kate, this man must really love you; that ring you're wearing cost a lot of money. Look at the size of those diamonds. You know, I know my jewelry, girl."

Rin looked down at the ring she was wearing, then looked up at Kevin and replied, "Thank you, Chioma. Yes, Kevin is very good to me."

Kevin said, "Good eye, Chioma, but your friend Kate here doesn't think that much of our wedding rings," showing his off as well.

"My goodness," Chioma said, "two rings? That must have set you back at least $50K or more. Not that I'm nosy or anything."

Chioma looked at them both and really seemed to like Kevin, not because of the rings, but because there was an aura of real love between them, and that was what Rin needed.

Kevin excused himself and went to get another drink.

Chioma whispered to Rin, "I think you'll be truly happy now. The way you look at him, Kate, the way he looks at you. I never saw that between you and Robert."

When Kevin returned, Rin asked Chioma, "What are you doing on the island?"

Chioma responded, "My son flew me here from Honolulu; he got this new private plane he likes to show off. You know how he is, Katie. He wants me to buy a piece from one of the artists for him. He could have purchased this piece anytime, but he wanted to buy it directly from the show. Makes no sense to me, but since I was on vacation in Honolulu, he asked me to come here. The things we do for our children. Anyway, I'm going back to Honolulu to continue my vacation tomorrow; I have some friends waiting for me. I wish we could get together for lunch tomorrow, Kate, but headed back in the morning. Please, let's stay in touch and get together as soon as possible. I miss you, my dear friend."

"I miss you too, Chioma, and we will."

They hugged again.

"Let's catch up soon," Chioma said, "and congratulations on that fine husband you have." She winked and added, "You two are indeed a beautiful couple. Continue to love her, Kevin. She deserves the best life has to offer. God bless you both."

Kevin waited until they left the gallery and then snapped, "Katherine, why didn't you tell me you were divorced? And it's been three years, for God's sake? How could you not tell me? How could you go through something like that without me? I don't understand. What the hell were you thinking?"

Rin replied, "Kevin, stop. Just stop. What were you going to do? It would just worry you and put you in some sort of mind set that you'd have to save me or something. You know those moods you get yourself into: 'I got to save my Rin,' or something. Please."

Kevin continued to vent his frustration and anger. He paced and waved his hands in the air. He was hurt, very hurt. He tried to compose himself, but out it came: "So, do you have a boyfriend now?

Is that why you didn't tell me? Are you sleeping with someone? Or are you and Robert still a thing? I can't believe this is happening; how could you not tell me?"

Rin snapped back, "Kevin, were you going to leave your wife? Would you actually leave Sarah? I don't think so. And I wouldn't allow that, even if you wanted to. Can we just stop talking about my divorce, please? Just stop because I'm getting really upset with you."

Rin knew she needed to help de-escalate this argument so they could at least make it back to the villa without a scene on a public street, especially on this beautiful island. Kevin wanted people to believe they were married, and this was an argument that needed to be private.

In a calm voice, she said, "Sweetheart, let's just not talk about it anymore for now; let's pretend you know nothing about my divorce just for now. We were having such a wonderful time."

Kevin replied, "You didn't answer me. So do you have a boyfriend at home? Is that it? You're sleeping with someone else, right? I just don't understand why you didn't tell me you left Robert." His voice began to rise again. "I can't believe you kept this from me."

Rin snapped, "What the hell are you talking about? Just stop talking to me. You should be ashamed of yourself; you have no right to what I do with my life. And the truth is, I didn't leave Robert; he left me. And even if I did have a boyfriend or was sleeping with someone, it's none of your business. Whatever my life's decisions are, they are mine to make, not yours. You're just being jealous, again. You can't be jealous of anything that I do. You have no right to be jealous."

Kevin yelled, "What do you mean, he left you? Do you want him back? What the hell is going on with you, Rin? Have all these years been a lie between us? Have I ached and pined over you for nothing? Do you really love me like you say?"

Rin was so angry, she could barely compose herself. But she knew she should have told him sooner; she really did.

Hoping to de-escalate this situation, she turned away so Kevin could not see her watery eyes and said softly, "Robert left me because I couldn't give him what he needed. Because he knew my heart was somewhere else. He knew I loved someone else, desperately loved someone else. And you know that person is you, Kevin. It's always been you. Although I gave Robert no reason to think I was with anyone else these past fifteen years, I just couldn't give him that emotion he needed. I threw myself into my work, and we barely saw each other, and toward the end of the marriage, we hadn't slept together in a very long time. I didn't want Blu to have divorced parents, so he was the one to call it quits. It was all as simple as that, sweetheart."

Kevin calmed down. She was right. He became beyond jealous when it came to her. She had the last word for now. He called another cab back to the villa, and nothing more was said on the way home.

Kevin realized the argument had gone too far. They said things they did not mean, horrible things. He and Rin had arguments before, but nothing like this. This was the worst. When they got back to the villa, Rin tried her best to unzip the orange dress, which she had once felt beautiful in. Now she just felt miserable and confined, just like the way Kevin made her feel. She struggled to remove that stupid dress. Kevin reached to help her unzip, still hurt by her secret. His voice was calmer, but he was clearly upset and hurt.

With the dress unzipped, she walked away in a huff to the bedroom and slammed the door; this time, she locked it. There she removed her makeup, put on one a comfortable T-shirt, and climbed into bed. She didn't care if Kevin slept on the couch; she had nothing more to say to him.

Chapter 48

Regrets

Neither of them could sleep that night, and that's an understatement. In the morning, Kevin knocked on the door; it was a familiar knock when he needed to talk. She recalled that same knock a few days ago and on her hotel room door, the night he said he loved her for the first time.

Kevin asked Rin if he could come in. He thought the door was locked and didn't try.

Rin said, "If you want to come in, the door is open." She had unlocked it earlier.

He came into the room with his shirt and shoes off, but still wearing the pants he wore to the gallery.

"Babe, please let's just talk. We both said a lot of things that were hateful and wrong, and I'm sorry. I'm very sorry for what I said and how I said it. But I'm not sorry for my disappointment that you did not tell me."

She said, "I'm sorry too; I planned to tell you about the divorce before the trip ended. I didn't mean for you to find out this way."

She chose not to share she was also planning to tell him they would never talk again after this trip. It still wasn't time.

Kevin moved closer to the bed but didn't go far enough to sit down. He continued by explaining the shock of it all, and of course he wanted to make sure she was okay. Did she need money? What about Blu? How did the divorce affect her daughter? Was Blu okay? Did she still have a relationship with her father? Was there anything he could do for her? There were so many questions.

Kevin wondered why Rin didn't tell him about the divorce. Everyone else knew about it, he was sure of that, but not him. They told each other everything, why didn't she tell him? Although he didn't say it to Rin, he also wondered if they could be together permanently, even though he knew she would never go along with that discussion right now. But he wanted her so bad, and this could be their chance. During the discussion, Kevin believed Rin understood his concerns, and she assured him how much she loved him. And he knew she was exhausted by the back-and-forth and wanted to give it a rest for now.

Rin ended the discussion by saying, "I understand, baby; you love me very much, and I feel the same, but let's not talk about it anymore. I'll give you as many answers as I can tomorrow. I promise. But please know, my reasons had everything to do with protecting you, mostly protecting you from yourself."

Keeping her voice calm, Rin continued, "By the way, sweetheart, what about these rings? You led me to believe they were cheap costume jewelry when you took them out of your pocket. I had no reason to think otherwise. How much did these rings really cost? Do you have the receipt?"

Kevin brought over the velvet jewelry boxes and receipt for the rings. Rin inspected the receipt. The wedding set cost over $45,000.

"Why? Why would you spend all this money on a game we're

playing? I understood you about the safety thing; I get it. But this is crazy."

"It's not a game to me, Rin. I've always wanted to marry you, and you absolutely know that. So this is a gift and a reminder of our time on this island. Please let me have this pleasure, please, babe." He reached for the pendant around Rin's neck and said, "Do you remember the week before your wedding, your marriage to Robert? Our last night together, when I gave you this pendant to remember me by?"

"Of course I do."

He continued, "Well, I had originally bought an engagement ring for you but exchanged it for this pendant. I had no intention of that being our last night. I was going to ask you not to marry Robert and to marry me. But it was something you said a few weeks earlier. You persuaded me you didn't want me to be part of your public life. You loved me, I was sure, but you seemed to think our worlds were too different for us to be together, that somehow, we wouldn't be able to make it. Do you remember those conversations about the racists in my family?"

She nodded.

"And do you remember the discussions about how you couldn't bring a white boy home to your family?"

She said, "Yes, but what does all this have to do with us now?"

Kevin continued, "I remember how we talked about the racists in my family. And yes, there are some horrible, prejudiced people in my family, and I have no excuses for them, but there are racists and people who discriminate in everyone's family. This world is upside down, and we've gone backwards for sure, but there are many in my family who would have grown to love you, Rin, if given the chance."

Rin responded, "Sweetheart, we never got that deep into your family beyond the racists; it's such a powerful situation to deal with, don't you think?"

Kevin said, "Yes, but you also told me I was 'that white boy, the white boy Kate was with,' and if we got married, I would have never been worthy of you by your friends or your family. I guess you were saying to me that you were an up-and-coming, beautiful, professional woman who would not settle for a white boy. That wouldn't fly in your world. Somehow you would have been a sell-out for not marrying your own kind. Don't you remember?"

Rin said, "I didn't mean it that way. I didn't mean it to come off that way. I think I was just pushing you away, because I didn't believe I was what you needed. I loved you so much, I wanted you to be happy. I was wrong."

He went on, "I understand you were not attracted to white men before you met me. And I'm grateful you gave me the chance to know you, to love you, and to receive your precious love back. That was one of my miracles in life."

She responded, "Thank you, sweetheart. I remember our lively discussions about politics too. You're center right, and I'm center left, but we never had a problem with that. We could have solved all the world's problems, given a chance."

He commented, "We did have some great debates regarding our political views. But getting back to us, what's serious here. These were all conversations led by you, not me. I gave few responses when it came to our future, but I remember everything you said. I listened to you, and I shouldn't have. I should have pushed back, but I didn't. So I exchanged the engagement ring for this diamond pendant. And I absolutely hate that I did. I wish I could go back and do it all over again."

Rin was overwhelmed by sadness and asked, "You were really planning to ask me to marry you that last night we spent together?"

"Yes, I was," he said forcefully. "Actually, I was prepared to beg you not to marry Robert. I wanted you as my wife more than anything in this world. I still do. But I let you convince me otherwise. And it was all my fault. I should have been more of a man and fought for you. But I wasn't sure what you wanted. I didn't know what to do.

"And there is one more thing I never told you." He put his hands on Rin's face to look at her straight in the eye and said, "Babe, I was at your wedding, standing in a side doorway when I watched you say, 'I do,' to Robert. I saw you hesitate, and then I wanted to stop the wedding like some cheesy movie." He smiled a moment and became serious again. "But I didn't, of course. I just let my heart sink in my chest and tried to keep back the tears. As close as we are, you've never seen me cry. But I cried over you." He removed his hands from Rin's face and continued, "Babe, I hurt for a long time; it was a constant dull ache that crushed me; it hung over me for months. That kind of hurt made me feel ill. I married, but I never got over you."

Rin's sadness increased as tears welled up in her eyes. She remembered exactly the way Kevin described those conversations. She had no idea he wanted to marry her, and she had no idea he was at the wedding. But she looked for him in the crowd. She had a crazy thought he would stop her as well.

Rin said those things to end the affair and push him away from her, so she could begin her marriage to Robert on a clean slate; she was so torn that last night they were together all those years ago. She didn't realize he was ready to fight for her if he had been given the chance. She finally told Kevin the truth. If he had asked her, she would have indeed married him and without question.

She said, "Baby, you don't know how much I wanted to hear those words that night. I wanted you more than anything in this world. I wanted to be with you for the rest of my life, and damn everyone else. I was ready for that fight. I didn't know you felt the same."

Kevin dropped his head in his hands; he was horrified that he didn't push back all those years ago. He looked up, and Rin was silently sobbing. He held her in his arms while she cried. He crawled into bed beside her with his pants still on and held her until she fell asleep. He couldn't sleep; he was still deeply hurt by what had transpired and all he had learned that day.

Day 9:
The Cat Suit

Chapter 49

A Day Apart

The next morning, Kevin still felt devastated she kept the divorce from him, although he understood her reasoning. But he had many other reasons for concern: the lack of honesty between them, her having to go through it without his consoling her, the reasons for the divorce, her well-being after the divorce, her financial situation, and what the divorce meant for their relationship moving forward.

But Kevin was most devastated about the mistakes they made those many years ago, the life together they missed out on. Here they were, in the last half of their lives and still without each other, and it didn't have to be this way. It was all his fault. He would make things right. He would leave Sarah and marry Rin. Sarah would be okay; she'd have all the money she needed, and the boys were grown up now. There would be no more excuses. He just must convince Rin. He knew she was her own woman, and he couldn't make her do what she didn't want to do. But she loved him, and that's for sure.

That morning, Rin put on a big act, trying to be cheerful. She even tried to get Kevin in a good mood with a few jokes. When she awakened, Kevin was still in bed with her, on top of the sheets, with his pants still on. She wanted to make love and reached for him.

She said, "Baby, let's get these pants off you."

Last night, they were too angry with each other, and things got even more intense. Kevin tried but couldn't get hard and gently pushed her away. There was too much on his mind. He wanted to talk more. He wanted to tell her he was leaving Sarah.

Rin knew exactly what he wanted to say, so she jumped in quickly. "Baby, my divorce will not impact our relationship in any way." She didn't have the heart to tell him about her true plans yet. She said, "Please don't leave Sarah; she absolutely needs you. It will kill her, Kevin. She would not survive without you."

Rin knew he made all the decisions in their marriage, paid all the bills, and provided her with everything she needed and when she needed it, including any and all emotional support.

She said, "I couldn't do that to her. I don't need you, Kevin, at least not like that. Sarah does not deserve another woman destroying her life. I just won't do it. I know you, sweetheart; my divorce would have tormented you every day. That's why I didn't tell you. You'd wonder who I was seeing, what I was doing. You would absolutely be jealous. You know you would. Just like you did yesterday. You went nuts."

He started to intervene, but Rin said, "Please let me finish. In your mind, you'd believe I'd be out there, getting into all kinds of trouble, not paying attention to my surroundings." She smiled. "You'd be looking for ways to leave Sarah just for me, and that would have been my biggest worry. Your mood swings would have made you crazy thinking about all this. I couldn't put you through that. I just couldn't. I didn't tell you because I love you."

Kevin quickly intervened and said, "Rin, that was a decision we should have both made together."

"No, Kevin," she replied gently, "this was my decision to make, and my decision alone."

She kept thinking about how to deal with what Kevin still didn't know, that she had decided they would not see each other again after their stay on the island; it would hurt him too deeply to disclose this now. It might be better to tell him after they got home. But she would not break up his marriage. She just would not do that. She wanted him more than the breath in her body. But she couldn't do that to him or the mother of his three boys.

She didn't feel like cooking breakfast that morning, but she asked Kevin if he wanted a cup of coffee. He said no, he wanted to take a walk and get his head on straight. Rin indicated she would go by Kai's house and take him out for breakfast, and they could get a cup of coffee later. She might even take Kai shopping, if Malia approved. After they both got ready for the day, Kevin gave Rin a peck on the cheek, and they went their separate ways.

Kevin decided to go sailing with some islanders and tourists he met on the island. It was a beautiful day, and maybe he and Rin needed to take some time away from each other that day. All he could think about was the possibility of a life together with his Rin. But how could he leave Sarah? She was a good woman, like Rin said, and it would kill her if he left. She was frail, both physically and emotionally. Sarah needed him to take care of her. She was not strong like Rin, strong and confident. Why was he comparing them? It was wrong. He cared about Sarah; he even loved her, he just was not in love with her. Rin made him feel things that could not be described; she made him weak, and she made him strong, all at the same time. He knew what it felt like to love a woman completely and to be loved sincerely and passionately because of Rin. She was the love of his life, and that would never change. And Sarah was his wife, but that could change.

He lost Rin once before, when she married Robert; he couldn't lose her again. He would have to figure out a way to handle all this and make Rin understand. But the one thing he wanted Rin to know about his concerns for her, she would never understand. She would be angry with him for even bringing it up. Rin would not do well alone; she needed someone in her life. Even though he lost her to Robert, he was happy Robert cared for her and established somewhat of a safe haven in her life.

Rin didn't know how beautiful she was, both inside and out. She never met a stranger; she was kind and generous with her time and resources to nearly everyone. Some men and women took that to mean something else, and that could bring unwanted trouble for her if she were alone. She had no brothers and sisters, no nieces and nephews. Her parents were now gone, and Blu was married. Rin had lots and lots of friends and some extended family, many who were close, but who would look out for her day-to-day? No one knew how vulnerable she could be, not even her family. No one knew Rin the way he did. As smart as she was and as brilliant and self-sufficient as she was, Rin was oblivious to her surroundings; she could be vulnerable.

Rin and Kai had a beautiful day together. They traveled to Lanai City; it was a Saturday, and there was lots to do. He held her hand most of the time as he looked up at her and smiled with his snaggle tooth. Rin had grown to love Kai and his mother and planned to help them financially after she got back home. She decided to set up a college fund for him as well. Kai was so proud to be walking around town with Ms. Katie and holding her hand. By this time, Rin already knew billionaire Larry Ellison was the majority owner of Lanai, the smallest inhabited island of Hawaii, but she found out he recently announced he had made Lanai his full-time home as well.

She thought, *It must be nice to be a billionaire with your own island, because this place is absolutely awesome.*

Rin thought about taking Kai on the ferry from Lanai to Maui; the ride was only an hour, but she didn't want to take Kai off the island without Malia's permission. Lanai City was very walkable; it's a planned plantation, and Dole Park in the center had lots to do. So there was really no need to go anywhere else with Kai that day. She bought him lunch, an ice cream cone, a few souvenirs, and a gift for him to give his mother. It was July, which is Lanai's warmest and driest month (except for that rainstorm the other day). Nevertheless, any time of the year, Lanai remains with comfortable temperatures, with the highs hovering in the mid-70s and lows lingering in the mid-60s. It was getting late, nearly time for dinner, and Rin took Kai home. As they walked back, Kai asked Rin to sing. She did and taught Kai to sing along to "Twinkle, twinkle, little star, how I wonder what you are."

Kai was tired, so Rin put him on her back the rest of the way home, and he fell asleep. As she walked, she thought about Kevin; he was never far away from her mind. There was a song that came to mind by the Deele, "Two Occasions." She started to sing softly as she thought of Kevin, "I only think of you on two occasions, that's day and night, I'd go for broke if I could be with you; only you can make it right." Rin was always thinking about the lyrics of songs that matched her moods or thoughts, especially songs from the 1960s, 1970s, and 1980s. They could have had a little boy like Kai, she thought. She loved Kevin more than he could possibly know, and everything she did (and will do from now on) was in his best interest. She would not destroy his life. She would be with him, but in the next lifetime.

Chapter 50

Rin's Style of Dress

Rin and Kevin reached the villa about the same time in the late afternoon. They missed each other and were truly glad to see one another. Rin knew Kevin wanted to talk more, but at least he seemed more relaxed and happier. They kissed with a lot more passion than earlier in the day and made plans to go to a beach café for dinner that night. They expected a somewhat older crowd because of the advertisement of 1970s music and were looking forward to it.

Kevin thought about everything Rin said earlier about him not leaving his wife. He understood the kind of person Rin was, just another reason why he loved her so much. But he had every intention of leaving Sarah when they got back. He could not go another year without Rin fully in his life. He would deal with that himself and limit those conversations with Rin. But he would not keep the divorce action from her, like she kept hers from him. But for now, he wanted to take his mind off his planned divorce from Sarah for a while and enjoy Rin. They had a few more days on the island, and he planned to enjoy them immensely with the woman he loved.

Kevin was always delighted by the way Rin dressed, from the very moment he met her. She wore flowy outfits on the island with lots of color: sundresses, wide-leg pants, sleeveless tops, and skirts with T-shirts; she was extremely sexy but left a lot to a man's imagination. Sometimes, she wore deep plunging necklines and dresses with splits up the leg and with high heels that made her look like a goddess, but always tasteful. When casual and running errands, she wore long shorts just above the knee with a tank top or T-shirt. At the beach, she wore one-piece bathing suits most of the time, with sarongs tied around her hips and butt, unless she was going into the water. Whatever she wore made both men and women do a double-take. She looked absolutely stunning in her clothes.

At the villa, Rin mainly wore large-fitting T-shirts that hit mid-thigh and nothing underneath, absolutely nothing underneath. Kevin loved her in those T-shirts. Now and then, she put on a sexy nighty, which drove him crazy, but those T-shirts were his favorite. She had a beautiful butt, rounded hips, small waist, and more than her share of breasts. Kevin would say to himself over and over, "Mother Nature and God himself spent a lot of time on Rin; she was one of their greatest achievements." He recalled that first morning together, Rin's breasts were still firm and full, and she would have to be careful that those large nipples didn't show through her tank tops and T-shirts.

Chapter 51

You Can't Wear That!

That evening, Kevin watched Rin put on a black bikini before their night out.

He said, "Rin, you can't wear that; you'd cause a riot." He said it jokingly, but in truth he meant it. He didn't want her to wear that bikini.

She said, "I'm not wearing this all by itself; I'm going to make it even sexier."

She pulled from her suitcase a cat suit to wear over the two-piece bathing suit. It was a see-through, black lace, tight form-fitting dress, so tight at the bottom, she had to take shorter steps. The panty part of the bathing suit underneath barely covered her front bottom and nearly none of her butt. The top of the suit barely covered her nipples, and the black lace overlay did nothing to hide any of her shape. She looked amazing, but Kevin didn't want her to wear it in public.

He repeated, "You'll still cause a riot in that outfit."

She had shared many pictures of her in that cat suit with Kevin. It was part of a game for if they ever saw each other again.

He said, "I thought this was something you were saving for us, babe, saving for me. Let's stay home tonight."

He moved her hands toward him so she could feel how hard he was getting, but Rin said, "Let's go out, baby. I'll take care of that thing when we get back. It will be fun. It will."

Kevin was skeptical about Rin going out dressed that way, and he was a little hurt by it too, that she would choose that particular outfit to wear. This was out of character for her; she never showed herself that way in public. He didn't understand what was happening.

But in Rin's mind, she was trying to break the ice from all that happened these past few days, just some harmless spicy fun, so she thought.

On the walk to the restaurant, she was extremely playful, skipping in front of Kevin, grabbing him to see if he was still hard, kissing him on the cheek, slipping her tongue in his ear. She was trying to create some spicy fun for them both to enjoy; they only had a few more days left on the island.

Kevin enjoyed seeing Rin like that but was still hurt by the fact she wore that outfit in public and so much of her beautiful body was on display. Nevertheless, she was so sexy and such a turn on, he had to smile at her behavior. When they arrived at the party, many women had risqué outfits on. So Kevin relaxed a bit about Rin's attire and enjoyed the scenery she provided.

Rin noticed Kevin was being a little quiet that night as well; so she sincerely gave him a lot of attention. She sat on his lap most of the time until it was time to have dinner, then she sat across the table from him. He was indeed an exceptionally handsome man. He was strong, brave, kind, smart, and all this with a beautiful heart and soul. She was so lucky to have had him in her life, no matter how long or how short that time would be.

That night, he wore black knee-length cargo shorts and a white tank top that showed off his gorgeous tan and beautiful, strong arms and muscular legs. To Rin, he was the sexiest man there; in fact, she thought he was the sexiest man alive.

She looked across the table from him and said, "Always remember, sweetheart, I'm so incredibly thankful for you; I can't even describe it. I will forever be grateful to God for gifting you to me for however long I have you."

Kevin thought what she said to him was beautiful, but again, there was something not said. Later in the evening, he couldn't wait to get back to the villa so they could make love. It was true that others were dressed just as risqué, but no other woman there had a body like Rin. She stood nearly a head taller than the others, and she seemed even taller with all that beautiful hair piled loosely on top of her head. She was always the most beautiful woman in any room, and he had to admit, in that outfit, she was stunning in the moonlight.

Chapter 52

The Drunk White Man

As they were preparing to leave, a Beach Boys song came on. This older drunk white man came over to Kevin and Rin's booth, eyed Rin up and down, and said, "Let's dance."

He looked at Kevin and said, "This is too much woman for just one man," and he started to pull her out of the booth. Rin raised her hand to Kevin to stay back, a gesture that she would handle the situation.

Rin slapped him hard. Then, the man called her a nigger and raised his hand to hit her. Before he could strike her, Kevin grabbed the man and threw him to the floor. He placed his knee on the man's chest and raised his fist to punch him in the face.

Rin screamed, "No, Kevin! He's not worth it. Please, let's go home, baby; let's go home".

Kevin leaned over to whisper in the man's ear. "If you ever touch my wife again, or if you look at her, I'll fucking kill you. Do you understand, man? I'll fucking kill you."

The restaurant staff and other patrons saw what happened and apologized to both Rin and Kevin. Most had come to know them and liked them very much.

Kevin and Rin began to walk home in silence.

After a minute, she said, "So I guess this is my fault, huh? You didn't want me to wear this outfit; just say it, Kevin. It's my fault."

He raised his voice just a bit and said, "Katherine, it's never a woman's fault when a man touches her without permission; it doesn't matter what she wears. That's not the issue. You could have been butt naked, and that man had no right to touch you. I scared myself tonight, babe; I wanted to kill him. I think for the first time, I could have killed somebody. That name he called you. He made me sick. The point to be made is that outfit was for me, no one else. You promised me numerous times when you sent me those pictures, it was for us. We've waited fifteen years to be together, and you decided to wear it for the whole world to see. Why, Rin? Why would you do that?"

"I don't know, sweetheart. I'm sorry, baby. I'm really sorry. I just wanted us to have fun tonight. I didn't mean to hurt you by wearing that outfit. I wanted us to forget about my divorce from Robert, forget about those stupid decisions we made when we were young. I should have told you about the divorce; I'm so sorry for that as well. I never meant for you to find out this way. I had planned to tell you at the end of our trip."

"Rin, I can't stay angry with you very long, I just can't. But we need to make plans on what we're doing next after we leave this island. I'm not saying we need to make immediate decisions, but we can't go on like this. I can't lose you; I just can't. I bought those rings because I wanted to be married to you and feel like your husband. Remember, we used to do this all the time when we travelled for work. Babe, I really think you'll be safer if people believe we're married.

She said, "But tonight, it didn't seem to make much of a difference to that fool."

Kevin replied, "It could have been a lot worse if you weren't perceived to be my wife. Would all those folks have stood up for us if you were just some woman I was travelling with? It's not a game to me, Rin, and it's not a game to you, and you know that."

She said, "Let's just enjoy the time we have left on this island. Please, Kevin, no more talk until we get home. That will give us both time to think and have clear heads for our next discussion. Don't you agree?"

Kevin reluctantly nodded. When they got to the villa, the cat suit came off. It didn't have the same meaning it had earlier; it had been tainted by their encounter with that drunken fool. They took a long warm bath together. They soaked in the tub and then headed to bed to make love. Kevin wanted to make up for not being able to perform earlier. They loved each other in those special ways, taking their time to make sure the other was satisfied.

It was always the same; when Kevin was inside of Rin, it was hot, it was warm, it was safe. His kisses were always sweet and caring. And they truly enjoyed each other's bodies in every way possible. Whenever he reached an orgasm with Rin, he was overwhelmed because of his love for her, but the sexual act was never over until he was sure Rin was satisfied. If someone asked him to explain it, he would say it was an ache that only Rin could ease.

She always felt a fullness and warmth with Kevin; it felt like an electric current working its way through her body, generating an indescribable ecstasy. She vowed that no other man would ever touch her again. Both felt a sense of euphoria as they went to bed in each other's arms, but neither slept and neither knew if the other slept. On both their minds was the future; neither knew the future the other had planned.

Day 10.
The Assault

Chapter 53

Kevin Realizes Rin Waited for Him

The next morning Kevin and Rin woke up to their usual morning routine. Kevin left early to buy some of Rin's favorite fruit for breakfast. During his walk, he thought about that first night with Rin on the island, and he realized she had not been with anyone else for a very long time. It was three years since the divorce, and Robert and Rin had not been together at least a year prior to that. So it was four years since she had been with a man. She didn't say, but he knew it to be true. She had not had sex in four years. He made a fool of himself by accusing her of having another boyfriend. He accused her because of his misguided jealousy, so stupid. He conceded to himself that jealousy was surely part of it, but most of it was not being with her, not being there for her when she needed him.

Kevin recalled how extremely tight she was that first night, when she put him inside her. He remembered not wanting to hurt her and trying to be as gentle as possible; that was partly why he asked her not to move when he was first inside her. He also was afraid of coming too quickly. And he remembered both the pleasure and pain she experienced during that night. It was like making love to a beautiful virgin. Did she save herself for him? For their time together on this beautiful island? Then he also remembered, Rin always made personal decisions in her own way and in her own time; she rarely asked anyone's opinion about what she should do in her personal life, not even his.

Kevin finally returned to the present when he heard Kai say, "Hi, Mr. Kevin." He was riding toward him on his bike.

"Hey, buddy," Kevin said. "Are you having breakfast with us this morning?"

Kai said, "Yes, Mr. Kevin, I'm headed to your house now."

"Okay, tell Ms. Katie I'm bringing all kinds of fruit, so she doesn't have to cook much. Maybe we'll have some fruit smoothies. What do you think about that?"

"Sounds good, Mr. Kevin, but I like bacon and eggs."

"So do I, but let's have these fruit smoothies with Ms. Katie this morning. This is her favorite. What you think?"

Kai said, "Okay," and rode off.

Chapter 54

Kai Saves Rin

Back at the villa, the drunk from the night before broke into the villa, just as Ren came out of the bathroom. She screamed at him to leave.

She yelled, "My husband will be back any minute."

The man said, "I've been watching your husband. I heard him say he'd be gone about an hour, so I have plenty of time to get what I want from you, you uppity nigger bitch. Who do you think you are, hitting me, you nigger bitch?" He grabbed a knife from the kitchen and headed toward her.

"Get out! Get out!" Rin shouted. She tightened her robe and looked for something to fight with. At that moment, Kai walked in the front door; he saw the screen door had been broken, which puzzled him. He yelled out for Ms. Katie.

"Ms. Katie! Are you here? Mr. Kevin said —" He suddenly saw the man at the bedroom door with the knife; Kai was frozen in place.

Rin saw him and yelled at Kai to run. But he didn't move; he must have been in shock.

She shouted frantically, "Kai, run! Run, Kai!"

The man turned to follow Kai with the knife. She shouted at the intruder, showing him part of her breast, "Is this what you want, you sick bastard? You sorry-ass piece of white-trash, better come and get it."

She was hoping to make him more angry so he wouldn't hurt Kai; now she was ready for a fight. He would not hurt that child.

Kai ran to his bike and rode like the wind to find Kevin, who was already headed back to the villa. For some reason, he decided to head back early and was only a few blocks away.

Kai screamed at the top of his lungs, "Help! A man is trying to hurt Ms. Katie. Help Ms. Katie." Kai was crying and shouted, "Please, Mr. Kevin, Ms. Katie needs you."

At first, Kevin didn't understand what Kai was saying, but he was clearly upset. Then he realized what Kai was saying; someone was hurting Rin. Kevin was a runner and broke all records in that sprint back to the villa. He ran much faster than Kai could ride his bike.

By the time Kevin got to the villa, the man had Rin pinned to the floor, but she was still fighting. Her robe was torn but it was still on; the man had not raped her yet, but he was getting the best of her. Kevin picked the man up with one hand and flung him to the other side of the room. Kevin flew into a rage as he proceeded to beat him and beat him and beat him, while the man begged for his life. He was no match for Kevin. Rin pleaded with Kevin to stop before he killed him. Kevin had already promised this man he would indeed kill him if he came near Rin again.

But Kevin didn't hear Rin's cries to stop. He took the knife out of the man's hand and started to stab him in the face, but at that very moment, he did hear Rin's voice.

"Baby, please, this man is unconscious; he may be dying. Look at all this blood."

Kevin stopped, but kept the knife in his hand; he was still thinking about killing him. He wanted to kill him. Then the police appeared with their guns drawn, and they told Kevin to drop the knife. Kai had brought the police. It was almost like they could hear what he was thinking.

After Kevin dropped the knife, he grabbed Rin and held her tight.

"Are you hurt, babe? Did he hurt you?" He saw blood where the man had cut her in various places and asked the police to send for an ambulance.

"I'm okay, sweetheart. I am."

Rin had small cuts on her arms from the knife and bruises from the fight, but nothing too serious.

Chapter 55

Rin Goes to the Hospital

R in and Kevin were escorted outside. There were lots of police cars and an ambulance. Rin was reluctant to go to the hospital to get checked out; Kevin couldn't convince her, and the paramedics couldn't convince her, either. So Kevin asked Kai to go get Dr. Shaw, the young doctor he befriended on the island; he was a tourist on his honeymoon. Kai knew where the doctor was staying.

When Dr. Shaw arrived, he checked Rin out thoroughly and suggested she go to the hospital for some routine tests and x-rays.

She said, "I was not raped, Doctor."

Kevin said it was true, he got there in time. But the doctor wanted to make sure she didn't have a concussion.

Kevin never left Rin's side at the hospital during all the exams, x rays, MRIs, and everything the nurses and doctors had to do to make sure she was okay.

He put his face in his hands once again and said, "I can't lose you, babe. I just can't. This has always been my biggest fear, that something would happen to you, and I wouldn't be there to protect you."

Rin said, "But you were there, sweetheart; you're always there.

You may not be there physically, but you're always with me in spirit and thought. You are a part of me, and that is how I make it. It's how I survive in this world; it's why I fight."

Kevin was half-listening to what Rin was saying; he was still playing the events in his mind. She could have been really hurt this time. She could have been raped or even killed.

He asked, "How did you hold him off all that time? It must have been about five minutes or longer."

"It was because of you, sweetheart; no other man will touch me like that except you. I would die first, before I let that happen. And I will fight to live as long as you're on this earth. It's because I love you that I was able to fight him off."

Rin was a spiritual person. She had decided not to see Kevin ever again because what they'd been doing all those years was a sin. She drew strength from God for this commitment. But she was also committed to her love for Kevin. Her mind, body, and soul were his and would always be his, even if they were across the globe from each other. Nothing could occur in her life that would change that.

Kevin then realized, for sure, that after her divorce, she had not been with any other man. But that was not important to him anymore; if she wanted to be with someone of her own free will, and she was safe, no problem. He could not control Rin, and that's what he loved about her most. But for now, he wanted to concentrate on what the doctors said.

They were at the hospital all day and into the evening. The doctors gave her a clean bill of health but said she might be a little sore for a few days from the bumps and bruises. They gave her a little something for the pain and assured Kevin she would be okay. Malia had cooked dinner for them and brought it over after they came home. After eating dinner and taking the pain medicine, Rin went right to sleep.

Chapter 56

Dr. Shaw's Visit

Later that evening, Dr. Shaw dropped by to check on Rin and review the pain medicine that was prescribed. He was pleased with what she was taking and her efforts for pain management. He was also pleased with the results of the tests that Kevin brought home. He had some questions for Rin himself but didn't want to wake her. The young doctor was a neurologist, and Kevin was grateful for his input. Kevin asked him if he would like a beer and stay awhile. He could use the company.

He said, "Sure. I could use a beer."

They sat at the kitchen table and began to chat.

The doctor said, "My wife often commented on how much you and your wife are in love, even after twenty-five years of marriage. She hopes we can still be that much in love after twenty-five years together."

Then he asked Kevin how the two had met.

Kevin said, "I first saw Rin in an office building lobby."

"Rin?" the young doctor said. "I thought your wife's name was Katherine. Never mind; KatheRINe; I get it."

"Yes, I'm the only one that calls her that." Kevin chuckled.

"That's a long story all by itself. I want to tell you all about how I met her though. I don't think I've shared the full details of our meeting to anyone before. I need to talk about my Rin, I really do." Kevin almost went into a trance as he recalled the first time he saw her. He closed his eyes and began to tell the young doctor his story.

"The first time I saw Rin, I had just got off the elevator from attending a very important meeting on the thirtieth floor of an office building. Time seemed to stand still all around me, except for her walking toward me from a distance away. She took long, confident strides in slow motion while everyone else around her seemed to stand still in place. It looked like an angel had arrived. She was the most beautiful woman I had ever seen.

"As we moved closer to each other on opposite sides of the lobby, she looked so beautiful. She had caramel-colored skin that was flawless and almond-shaped big brown eyes. Her skin was an amazing color, I noticed. She wore very little makeup and just a tad of lipstick. She wore an off-white linen suit with a pencil skirt that landed just above her knee. It fit her perfectly, I thought, with the black satin blouse she wore underneath. I remember every detail of what she wore as if it was yesterday.

"Her bare legs were shaped perfectly for those black high heels she wore. Her hair was very long, tightly swept back into a ponytail that nearly hit her waist. She was very tall, at least six feet in those high heels."

Chapter 57

Kevin Continues…the First Time He Saw Rin

K evin paused a moment to smile.

"She was slim, but not skinny at all. There appeared to be a very shapely body under that suit. She moved with such style and grace, and with noticeable sophistication that I had not seen in a long while. In those heels, I noticed she was a head taller than all the women around her and taller than most of the men.

"As we moved even closer together in the crowd, just a foot or so away from each other, I still couldn't take my eyes off her. She was briefly looking away, and when she looked my way, our eyes locked. Because she wore her hair in a ponytail, I was able to see every aspect of her face. She took my breath away, and I had to remind myself to breathe. I had never had such a powerful emotional reaction to any other beautiful woman. She made me feel wonderful, just to be in her presence.

"Not only was she beautiful, but she was also sensual and sexual in her manner. Not in the way one would think. I'm not talking about 'I wanted to tap that.' Or 'I wish I could get me some of that.' Not then, at least."

Kevin had to laugh as he paused a moment to think about their sex life.

"I thought of her as a woman that was awe-inspiring, and I wanted to know her, to be near her. She displayed such confidence, a woman who knew her own unique energy. However, she seemed unaware of her surroundings, and the affect she had on those around her, the second glances by both men and women. I had the overwhelming desire to protect her. You probably wonder how I could tell all that in such a short encounter. I could tell, and I knew I needed to know more about her. I just wanted to be near her, even if it was for just one more moment.

"But then I caught myself and came back to reality. This tall, elegant, exquisite beauty had a young face; she couldn't have been no more than sixteen or seventeen years old, I thought. Her face reminded me of a gorgeous teenage actress, like Brooke Shields.

"I said to myself, 'Kevin, this is jailbait; be careful.' At that moment, I realized she was a woman of color. I had not noticed this before; she only appeared as an angel dressed in white. But I got to tell you, man; no actress could compare to my Rin's beauty, and I felt her gentle and peaceful spirit immediately.

"But then I thought further about how she was dressed, her confidence, and the bag she carried, as if she was attending an important meeting. Maybe she was a college intern or something. She must be at least eighteen. I was nearly twenty-five then, and eighteen was too young for me to consider. But I had to know. So I ran after her and caught up with her as she entered the elevator, apologizing to those I nearly knocked over along the way.

"I got into the elevator and noticed the button for the thirtieth floor was lit up, so I didn't press the keys for any other floor. I just came from that floor myself. So I proceeded to talk about the weather, and she looked at me and smiled; oh, what a pretty smile she had. She had perfect white teeth, and everything was affected by that smile; her almond-shaped eyes just lit up.

"She didn't say much, but I gathered she was an attorney for the firm I was hoping to do business with. So now I knew she had to be in her mid-twenties. What a relief. I was grateful I had that short time with her alone. No one got on or off the elevator as we rode to the thirtieth floor. So I had time to be alone in her presence, just the two of us. Although she had the face of a beautiful young girl, she showed so much maturity in her demeanor. Our conversation consisted of short sentences and one-word comments, but we never stopped looking at each other. She seemed to be interested in my babbling. I introduced myself, and she said her name was Katherine. I repeated every syllable back to her: 'Kath-e-rine, what a beautiful name,' I said.

"The elevator stopped, and she got off. I was afraid to ask for her phone number or give her mine. I didn't want to be too forward; she may have rejected me, and I would have been devastated. Who was I to think this magnificent creature could really be interested in me? But I knew I would see her again. I would make that happen.

"I rode the elevator back down to the lobby, whispering her name over and over to myself, but 'Kath-e-rine' was too long; I decided to call her 'Rin.' I would see Rin again tomorrow, if I could make that happen. I told myself I would take it slow, be a friend first; I didn't want to scare her away. In time, I hoped she would begin to want me in her life somehow, as much as I wanted her in mine right at that very moment.

"Man, I thought, I was being stupid. I didn't even know her, and I could see spending the rest of my life with her. And you know what else? I never told Rin what it was like for me when I first met her, but I should have."

The doctor asked, "What made you go after her? What really drove you to run to that elevator?"

Kevin said, "When you see something that beautiful, you want to see it again, get a closer look. And what I found on that elevator is that Mother Nature, maybe God, saw fit to put a lot of time in this one woman. She was perfect to me. She was not only beautiful, but I could see her strength, confidence, grace, and kindness, even though not much was said between us. I could feel a connection in a moment in time; I was sure she felt something from our encounter as well."

Kevin went on to admit, "To this day, Rin doesn't know that the meeting that was called the next day was at my request. It turned out the client she was meeting was my client as well. She was called in to review the contracts I submitted for a bid on commercial construction. The next day, we were formally introduced in that meeting, and we both acknowledged our previous encounter on the elevator. I held her hand a little longer than I should, but touching her brought me so much joy; it was like touching an angel. I told myself, *Breathe, Kevin, remember to breathe.* And the rest is history."

The doctor assured Kevin that Rin was fine, and by morning, she would be herself, and they could make plans for their day. He said to give him a call if anything was different. However, he thought it might be best that both get counseling after a horrific event like that. Kevin reluctantly agreed that he needed it, but he would surely talk to Rin about getting counseling. Attempted rape is serious, and he suggested Rin talk to a professional.

Day 11.
Ferry Ride
to Maui

Chapter 58

Rin Worries about Kai

R in woke up well rested, feeling pretty good, but a little sore. She thought the best thing to do was to take a hot shower and get some exercise and fresh air. It was their last full day on the island.

Kevin told Rin he had spoken with Malia. He said, "Kai wanted to check on you, but his mom thought you needed the rest, and we could use some time alone. Malia is right, but I know you want to see him; you're worried about him, right? What he saw?"

"Yes, I am," Rin said. "I've grown fond of that little boy."

"So have I, babe. He saved your life, you know."

"I know," she said, smiling.

Kevin asked Rin if she'd like to take the ferry ride from Lanai to Maui. She thought that was a great idea. She also wanted to cook a small breakfast, but he had brought back bagels and cream cheese. Neither of them had ever been to Maui, and they looked forward to the trip; it was about an hour each way. Maui, known also as the Valley Isle, was the second largest Hawaiian island. The island was beloved for its world-famous beaches, the sacred ʻĪao Valley, views of migrating humpback whales, farm-to-table cuisine, and the magnificent sunrise and sunset from Haleakalā. It's not surprising Maui has been voted best island in the U.S. by *Condé Nast Traveler* readers for more than twenty years.

So true to Rin's habits, she packed sunscreen, a blanket, snacks, water, and light jackets in one of her boho bags for the ferry ride and their exploration of Maui. They planned to have lunch and visit one of Maui's most famous beaches. On this trip, Kevin gladly carried that bag, with a smile. Rin wore a long halter sundress along with flat sandals. She also had on a beautiful straw hat and sunglasses. Kevin wore loose-fitting linen pants with a drawstring and a tank top, as well as sunglasses and sandals. They were both comfortable for the trip, yet still a stunning couple.

Chapter 59

Seeing Sam again

The ferry ride to Maui was beautiful; the weather was perfect, sunny, and clear. Kevin and Rin held hands or had their arms around each other the entire trip. She leaned back against him for comfort during most of the ride. His body was always so comfortable for her. Kevin wondered if they would run into someone they knew. Maui was a more commercial, less reclusive island, and he was still married. He wanted to tell Sarah of his decision; he didn't want her to hear it from anyone but him. Those worries quickly went away as Rin leaned against him. Kevin didn't care anymore about seeing anyone they knew; Rin was his wife.

Rin had braided her hair into one long braid that hung halfway down her back. She looked very pretty with the braid, hat, and sunglasses. It reminded him of when he first met her, that long ponytail down her back. Rin had always been a beautiful woman, but today, she looked like a lovely, sweet young girl, like when they met. Kevin never tired of looking at her; however, he was waiting to hear someone say, "Who's the old man with that young girl?" Kevin and Rin were not that far apart in age, but most would assume he was older. Rin had such a youthful look, while Kevin was completely gray.

After reaching Maui, they found a casual restaurant to have lunch and a couple of drinks. Maui's culture is rooted in Hawaiian traditions: the Aloha spirit, the Hawaiian language, hula dancers, surfing, and the beauty and spirit of the land. Western explorers arrived in Hawaii using modern tools of navigation and sailing. They arrived in Hawaii as sandalwood traders, whalers, and missionaries. Kevin thought Maui was boisterous, gregarious, and mischievous; he loved it.

Maui rose out of the depths of the Pacific Ocean in the shape of a figure-eight. The island's dimensions were owed to a pair of massive shield volcanoes that erupted about the same time. The two largest and most popular visitor destinations, offering the most accommodation options, were West Maui and South Maui. However, the pair chose a quaint town within a resort community to explore; it would be safer for keeping their secret than the popular destinations.

Nevertheless, the Maui Gods were against them. In that quaint old town, they ran into someone they knew; his name was Sam. Sam was one of the first subcontractors Kevin hired, and they became colleagues and work friends back in the day.

While walking hand in hand along the commercial shops, they both heard someone call out, "Kevin! Kate!"

When they turned around, a man and woman were running toward them. Kevin and Rin stiffened and looked at each other, not sure how to best handle the situation. And they were holding hands as well and didn't want to suddenly pull away.

It was Sam. He said, "It's such a surprise to see you both. It's been nearly twenty-five years; you two have not changed at bit." He looked at the rings on their fingers and said, "I knew you two were going to get married back then. Kate, I could tell Kevin was crazy about you before he knew it himself. I bet you've been married a long time. I bet it's been a lot of years. Kate, one evening after a long workday, I told Kevin you should be his woman. He said you were engaged at the time, but I see that Kevin changed your mind, and you married him instead."

Sam wore a big grin and kept talking and talking and talking.

Finally, he said, "Oh, by the way, this is my wife, Jennie. Sorry, babe, I'm just so excited to see these two."

Rin and Kevin looked at each other, just nodded, and smiled at Sam.

Kevin finally got a word in: "We're so glad to see you, Sam, and that you're doing well."

Sam said, "Why don't we all have dinner together tonight, here on Maui?"

Kevin said, "Maybe the next time; we're leaving tomorrow to go home."

They talked a little longer, exchanged numbers with Sam, and said their goodbyes. They had dodged a bullet for that one second.

Rin said to Kevin, "I wonder if Sam was able to find out the truth."

Kevin responded, "I really don't think so, but it doesn't matter now."

Rin gave Kevin a puzzled look; he knew she would and decided not to return the glance.

Chapter 60

The Magnificent Tree

They headed to the beach to spend some time there before the ferry ride back to Lanai. Maui's beach was so romantic. They gazed at the beautiful creatures that hovered all over the beach and on the deep seawaters. There were many beautiful birds that flew all over the shore and ocean. Their colored feathers brightened the sea and looked marvelous when illuminated by the sun's rays. They were gorgeous.

The beach sand was golden and bright and gleamed near the water. The beach was charming, cozy, elegant, exciting, tranquil, and vibrant, all at the same time. Kevin and Rin shared a kissed but needed more. It was the most romantic place they had ever seen, and they walked away from the shore toward a small forest of trees; they walked farther until they felt the crunch of leaves under their bare feet. The wind whistled through the trees, and the trees smelled damp, as they were near the water.

They came upon the most beautiful tree of all; it was extremely large and surrounded by wildflowers and other greenery; birds were singing above. The tree could have been a thousand years old. Kevin had his pocketknife and decided to carve their names in the tree trunk; it seemed like a silly idea to him, but Rin thought it was romantic.

Kevin said, "I'm too old to be doing this, but it feels good, Rin; it feels right, for some reason. It makes me feel like a teenager." He carved "Kevin + Rin" in that magnificent tree.

Rin turned her back to Kevin so she could run her fingers across their names.

As she caressed their names carved in the wood, Kevin removed her hat and sunglasses, and then unbraided her hair. He then ran his fingers through her hair to ensure its fullness. At that moment, he didn't want Rin to look like a girl; he wanted her to look like his woman, a woman he loved very much. Then he put his arm around her, just above her waist and just below her breasts, and put his other hand on top of Rin's as she traced their names in the tree.

He kissed her neck tenderly and said, "I love you, Rin. I love you. Are you okay, babe? Is there something I can do to help you? Are we okay together, here in this place? Do you still want me after all you've been through?"

He had so many questions, but Rin answered only one: "Do I still want you after all I've been through?" She whispered, "Yes, baby, I want you. I will always want you."

Chapter 61

Making Love in Maui's Beauty

Kevin pressed his body up against hers, but gently. He held her close by bracing her against him with his arms wrapped around her. He braced them both from the tree by keeping his other hand up against the tree near where their names were carved. With love and tenderness, he kissed Rin's neck, her ears, her cheeks, anything he could reach from behind. He wanted to be as gentle as possible after all she had been through. As he continued to embrace her tenderly, he grew harder and harder.

Kevin wanted to be sure this is what she wanted, so he waited until she was ready. She raised her dress and removed her panties; she smiled as Kevin continued moving gently against her body. She moved her body forward toward the tree while reaching around for him, but he kept her upright and straight up against him. Rin arched her back, instead. He didn't want rough, doggy-style sex. He wanted to love her tenderly, not just sex.

He loosened the drawstring of his pants to give him some slack ; he removed himself and touched Rin as to how he would reach her in that upright position. She arched her back, and it was easy for him to place himself completely and fully inside her. Penetrating her from behind was especially hot and gave him his deepest penetration. It also allowed him to control the pace of their lovemaking to make sure she was okay. He wanted her to feel his love while they were in the beauty of this place.

When he finally entered her, he moaned louder than he expected, and she sighed with a short breath quietly. He began slow strokes, very slow, while never letting go of the tender embrace he had on her. She moved with him in absolute delight as he continued to hold her upright against him. He thought he could never let her go, for any reason; he could be with Rin forever, just as they were at that moment. He loved her so much.

Rin could see the beautiful water, the birds that flew above the water, and gorgeous humpback whales in the water. She could see the beauty of the greenery and the flowers, and in the distance, the beach. She began to come, and with each orgasm, she closed her eyes to relish it.

She opened her eyes again and whispered to Kevin, "Look, baby; can you see all this beauty?"

He looked for a second but wanted to concentrate on Rin. His main priority was not to hurt her and to make her feel good about being with him. She reached back to hold his hips to keep up with his rhythm. But she noticed something different with Kevin this time. When he came, he usually performed faster strokes so she could always tell when it was about to happen. This time, he was slow and easy the entire time, sensual and sweet, more loving than ever, and she could only tell he finished when his moans stopped. She realized he didn't want to hurt her.

He did not release his embrace of her right away. He held her for a while longer to share in the beauty of the scenery. The beach and the forest were enchanting and made way for a special togetherness in that moment. Rin told herself she would remember being with Kevin in this beautiful place. She would remember this forever, even into their next lifetime.

As dusk arrived, Rin turned around and gave Kevin one of those lingering kisses he loved. That kiss proved to him that Rin would be able to deal with the assault. But he would make sure she got counseling.

They straightened their clothes and headed for the ferry, hand in hand during a beautiful sunset. Neither said anything on the way back; they just looked at each other, smiling and holding hands, or Kevin's arms were around Rin's waist. It was their moment in time to remember, always.

Day 12.
The Last Day

Chapter 62

Time to Leave Lanai

K evin and Rin lay in bed as long as they could before it was time to get up and pack. Kevin did most of the talking about what they should do next, nothing for sure, but he wanted to discuss how to move forward and build their life together.

Rin just listened and nodded. She didn't have much to contribute to the conversation. She didn't want any arguments on their last day. He was excited and also concerned about their future, but he was sure they would have a future together. He would make that happen. They would make that happen together.

They noticed they had not heard from Kai; they assumed he would have breakfast with them on this last morning. Kevin suspected his mother may have wanted him to give them some privacy and suggested they stop to see them before they left. After they had a quick breakfast, they went to visit Kai and Malia to say goodbye.

Rin wanted their mailing information so she could send them financial help and set up a college fund for Kai. She discussed it with Kevin, and he wanted to help as well. In fact, Rin had to put him in check because Kevin wanted to take over that whole college fund idea. She understood how he felt; Kai had saved her life, as far as he was concerned, and there was nothing that could repay him for that.

Their first flight was scheduled late in the afternoon; their connecting flights to get home were at different times. Rin purposely scheduled that last leg on separate flights, even though they were flying home to the same airport. Rin's flight left later than Kevin's. He didn't understand that. It would have given them more time to talk. However, Rin wanted to be alone on that last leg of the trip. She needed to think of how best to break it off with Kevin. She needed to think about what she would say and how she would stick to it. These twelve days in Lanai with him were more beautiful and wonderful than she could imagine. It would sustain her for the rest of her life. It would have to.

The Past to Their Future

Chapter 63

Rin Breaks It off with Kevin

Rin stayed true to her promise to God and her promise to herself. She called Kevin on the phone two days after they returned home and told him they could never see each other or speak on the phone again, and she explained why in detail. She told him it was over, and it was for the best. She gave him all her reasons, told him they had sinned and needed to get right with God, said she didn't want to hurt Sarah, and added that Sarah didn't deserve to be divorced. She spoke about the wonderful time they had in Lanai and said those memories would stay in her heart forever. They would sustain them, she believed. She didn't want to hurt Kevin; it would hurt her to not be with him, but it had to be. The next lifetime was at stake. She would get them to the next lifetime. Kevin was still married; somehow, he would have to move on.

Kevin was horrified. He was ready to leave Sarah but thought, at the very least, they could continue to keep in touch, talk on the phone, and text like they did before, at least keep up with each other's lives. As Rin spoke on the phone, he felt the same pain he had when she married Robert. It was blinding this time because he had hope. He would change her mind somehow. They took a break once before and got back together. He would not accept this as long term. Rin loved him.

Rin thought about writing Kevin a letter to further explain her decision, but instead, she wrote him a poem that flowed from her heart. It was easy because she loved him so much; she ached for him. The poem expressed the intensity of her love for him and their love for each other. She had to put what she was feeling on paper for them both to remember.

She didn't think Kevin understood why she never showed jealousy or guilt about their relationship. She believed there was no need to be jealous of Kevin's wife or any other woman who looked at him; she knew Kevin loved her all those many years. And if she let him, she would be first in his life. Although she may have had some doubts about the seriousness of his feelings in the very beginning, over twenty-five years ago, she knew now they should have been together. Kevin wanted that too. She had so many of her questions answered on that trip.

Throughout these many years, Rin prayed every day for three things: 1) for God to manage her guilt because she knew what she and Kevin did all those years was wrong; 2) for God to forgive her for loving this man so much; 3) and for God to give her the strength to leave him for the rest of this lifetime.

She thought about the lyrics to Deniece Williams's song *Black Butterfly*. This helped her be strong:

> Let the current lift your heart and send it soaring
> Write the timeless message clear across the sky
> So that all of us can read it and remember when we
> need it
> That a dream conceived in truth can never die
> Butterfly.

Chapter 64

Rin's Thoughts About Kevin's Wife, Sarah

R in would not accept Kevin leaving Sarah, for all the reasons she told him on the island. They discussed it over and over. Sarah was still totally dependent on him. She never worked outside of the home, but she did a wonderful job raising his kids and keeping his home the way he liked it; she was his pretty and dutiful housewife. That was a job in itself, and there was no shame in it. If Rin was married to Kevin, life would have been totally different for him. She was an independent, successful professional with her own law firm, her own ideas, and her own way of doing things. She was her own person and a handful to deal with.

This was not to say one way was good or bad regarding the career choices women make, but this was the life Rin chose for herself, which was a different kind of life than what Kevin was used to, when it came to living with a woman. She made her peace about leaving Kevin; it took every ounce of her entire being. She never loved anyone as much as she loved him. Every day, she ached to feel his touch, hear his voice, or just look at him. It was a horrible ache, but she would learn to live with it.

Rin kept coming back to Sarah in her thoughts. She knew Sarah would be devastated to lose Kevin, and she could not be the cause of all that hurt; all that pain would be her fault. She would not break up another woman's marriage. She recalled a time when Sarah threatened to commit suicide over something Kevin did. To Rin, it was such a little thing. It had something to do with his missing an important engagement she didn't want to go to alone. She thanked God it had nothing to do with her. Kevin called Rin immediately; she didn't have any real advice for him but told him to take it seriously and get her some help. Suicide threats should not be taken lightly. Rin thought she should have just slapped him upside the head and kept it moving. That's what she would have done.

But Sarah was frail and needed Kevin to do everything for her. Although they didn't think Sarah knew about Rin, they both believed she was capable of committing suicide, which is such a final act. During that horrible time for them both, Rin encouraged Kevin to help her and be there for her. But now that the two of the boys had left home and the youngest was leaving soon, Sarah's dependence on Kevin seemed to increase tremendously. Rin thought it must be suffocating for him. But this was his life now, and there was nothing either of them could do about it.

Rin's split from Robert was amicable. She just couldn't give him what he needed emotionally, although she tried. She really tried. Sex with Robert was adequate, but he couldn't satisfy her. No one would be able to satisfy her like Kevin, and at this point, she preferred no sex in her life if it couldn't be with Kevin. That was her promise to herself. It was not only the sex and lovemaking with Kevin, but it was also everything about him: his laughter, his smile, his voice, his walk, the way he looked at her, his eyes, his jokes, his mannerisms, the things they did together. It was everything about him that she loved.

She loved his goals in life, their similarities and differences, the things they had in common, and his instincts about her. He knew her better than anyone. And even if she never told him, she enjoyed the protection and security Kevin provided her and the instincts that surrounded those intuitions for her protection. He made her happy. He made her steady. Robert deserved someone who could love him the same way. Rin just couldn't do it. Rin knew it was because of Kevin. If Kevin was not a significant part of her life, she would never have known what this kind of love could be, and she and Robert would still be married today. But Kevin was part of who she was, and without him, she would prefer not to have an intimate relationship with any other man. It's impossible to achieve what she had, so she was prepared to do without.

Chapter 65

Rin's Marriage of Convenience

Rin dated several eligible bachelors during those three years she was single, and she continued to date after she and Kevin broke it off, but there was no sex involved. She didn't even kiss them on the lips. She barely let a man kiss her cheek to say hello or goodbye. After a while, she just got tired of dating and truly tired of men who just wanted sex; some wanted more of relationship, but she didn't want that, either. Some of them made her cringe.

But she did develop a mutual friendship with a man about ten years her senior; his name was Daniel. She cared about him like a brother. There was no emotional connection or any sexual desire. They were just good friends and enjoyed many of the same things. He was a very wealthy African American businessman but had never been married; many people thought he was gay. Rin just thought he was asexual ("a lack of sexual attraction to others, or low or absent interest in or desire for sexual activity"). They had known each other for many years and had grown to be good friends; she served as his lead attorney for many of his business transactions and always had his best interest in mind. Daniel was the perfect companion. However, he never knew about Kevin. No one knew about Kevin; Rin never told anyone.

Because of Daniel and Rin were only companions, she had time to think of Kevin every day; remembering him brought her orgasms from her many wonderful memories of their sex life: making love or just talking dirty when they couldn't be together. Even their arguments were marvelous to remember; they gave her peace and joy. Rin's memories made the present seem real; she just closed her eyes, and Kevin was with her each and every day. It was strange, but those memories strengthened her sense of identity and purpose, and the bond of their past connection was an important part of her present happiness. But she could not and would not see him.

Finally, Daniel asked her to marry him, and she agreed. She married him for convenience. Kevin was right, to some extent: Although she was independent and successful, she was not comfortable in the dating world, being single and sought after for nonsense. Or being pursued by someone she had no interest in. Some men she dated thought she would take care of them financially, and others thought she was just too independent. She wasn't attracted to other white men or any other man outside her race. In fact, she had not encountered any man she was attracted to. She had no interest. Kevin was her soul mate.

Rin had learned a lot while she was single; she depended completely on herself regarding her surroundings, who was a friend, and who was not. The world was not as it was growing up, and it felt like few could be trusted these days. She didn't like it, so being married to a friend helped shield her from all that. It was comforting; it was a safe and pleasant life filled with things to do and sincere friendship.

To be clear, Rin did not marry Daniel for protection; she often protected him from those who wanted to take advantage of him. Rin had wealth of her own, so this marriage was not about money. Some younger women even thought they could come between them to get Daniel's money; it was all so funny to Rin. She married Daniel for companionship, mutual respect, friendship, and no drama; this arrangement served them both very well. Daniel had no interest in women. And he always treated her much like a sister.

Rin was safe in her thoughts about Kevin; she missed him very much. She loved him with an ache that would remain for the rest of her life.

So after Kevin and Rin returned from the island and had that awful conversation, she blocked his number from her cell phone and decided to move out of the country; she was headed to London. Her firm had established a small office there that dealt with international contract law. All these years, Rin and Kevin only lived forty miles from each other; now they would be across the globe from one another. They knew where each other lived and raised their families; that was not a secret. Rin never went anywhere near Kevin's neighborhood; however, she was confident he had driven by her house on several occasions.

Kevin desperately tried to contact Rin over and over again. She didn't answer his calls, and her home was now vacant. By this time, he had received the poem Rin wrote; he read it nearly every day of his life, so he knew she still loved him. Rin's handwriting was beautiful (it reminded him of calligraphy), another one of her many talents. So this added to the gift she had given him to remember what they meant to each other.

Rin's law firm would not tell him how to contact her, so he continued to leave messages; there were strict instructions not to let anyone know where she was. Callers were told to leave a message, and she would reply if there was a need. Over the years, Rin received several calls from her US firm about messages from Kevin; she refused to call him back. It had to be over; it just had to be.

Chapter 66

Kevin Meets Rinda Blue, Rin's Daughter

About eight years after their trip to Hawaii, Kevin's wife passed away from breast cancer. He did everything he could to make Sarah comfortable during her illness. He took off work to care for her himself, along with professional nurses and caregivers. He wanted to be with her as much as possible. Their sons had their own lives and families to contend with, and he did not want to put that burden and responsibility on them.

Sarah's passing hurt Kevin deeply. To keep busy, he went back to running his mega successful development business; he lived alone and was finally contemplating retirement. He had no idea if Rin knew about Sarah's passing. She never contacted him.

Kevin had done very well and had become somewhat famous for his projects all over the world. Rin kept up with his successes and was so proud of him. Her law firm still did some specialized work for Kevin's company, but she was never involved. She had retired a few years ago and never heard about Sarah passing away.

About a year after Sarah passed, Kevin was in a trendy coffee shop near his office when he overheard a man say, "Rin, take your time; I'll be in the car with the kids."

He looked up to see a young woman who looked exactly like his Rin, just a little shorter, a tad slimmer, and darker in skin color. She was very beautiful, with Rin's face, Rin's hair, and Rin's confidence and grace: the spitting image of his Rin. He was blissful and at the same time confused. But it made Kevin positively happy to see a mirror image of the woman he loved.

Kevin walked over to her and said, "Is your name Rin? That's an unusual and beautiful name."

The young woman said, "My name is actually Rinda Blu."

He recalled Rin referring to her daughter as Blu; he never knew she named her Rinda.

"Is your mother's name Katherine? My name is Kevin, and you look just like her."

Rinda Blu replied, "Yes, my mother's name is Katherine. And if you say I look like her, then that's a really big compliment. My mother is very beautiful."

Kevin said, "Yes, I know. I remember how lovely your mother was, and I'm sure she's still very lovely today."

The young woman smiled and said, "She sure is."

Kevin continued, "I'm an old friend of your mother's. Did your mother call you Rin?"

Rinda Blu replied, "Yes, my mother loved the name Rin, and blue is one of her favorite colors. So she named me Rinda Blu."

Kevin immediately recalled the blue nightgown Rin wore on their first night on Lanai.

Rinda Blu went on to explain the meaning of the name and said it was very important to her. Her mother confessed a special person in her life told her about the name's Japanese origin.

"The name Rin means so much to my mom; she said it was part

of who she is, and it's imbedded in her soul. The name makes her
very, very happy, so she calls me Rin for short. She only calls me
'Rinda Blue' when she's a little angry with me. She always smiles
when she calls me just Rin."

Kevin asked, "Where is your mom these days? How is she?"

His heart sank when Rinda Blu answered, "My mother is doing
great; she lives in London with her new husband. She married my
stepfather, Daniel, about five years ago."

He could have fainted when he heard Rin was married again.
He could barely speak.

But he mustered up the courage to give Rinda Blu his phone
number and asked her to share it with her mom. "I would like to
truly hear from my old friend."

Rinda Blu said she would let her know; in fact, she planned
to talk to her mom later that day. She felt a connection to this
man somehow; he and her mother were very close at one time.
It compelled her to continue her conversation with this stranger.
But he didn't seem to be a stranger at all. He was a very handsome
and kind older man, and she detected a sadness about him, a
disappointment in his heart; he looked defeated somehow. She
wished she could do something to help him or say something that
would ease his sadness. She hated to end the conversation but
explained that her husband and children were waiting for her in
the car.

Kevin said, "Was that your husband who shouted your name?"
She said, "Yes."

"I'm happy he did," he said. "I looked up, and now I had a
chance to meet Katherine's daughter."

They shook hands, and she promised she would give her mom
his phone number that day.

Chapter 67

Kevin Recalls when Rinda Blu Was Born

As Rinda Blu left the coffee shop, she looked back and saw Kevin pull out a chain from around his neck. It had a ring on it. He kissed it, caressed it, and placed it back in his shirt, and then took a sip of his coffee. Even from afar, the ring looked familiar, but she put no more thought to it at that moment. She couldn't shake away the connection they had.

She called her mother later and gave her the phone number, asking her about who the man was, especially since it was her name "Rin" that drew him to her. But her mom wouldn't say much. She just said Kevin was an old friend, like he said. Rinda Blu always felt her mom had a secret. Could this man, Kevin, be that secret?

Kevin recalled the first time he saw Rinda Blu as a baby. It was in the hospital when she was first born. Rinda Blu would have to be in her late thirties by now, although she looked a lot younger. He saw her in Rin's arms in the hospital room those many years ago. He chose not to intrude, but he really wanted to enter the room and give them both a kiss. It would not have been appropriate; it took everything he had in him not to enter that room. It was one of the

most beautiful visions of Rin that he remembered, holding her new
baby and singing the sweetest lullaby with that beautiful voice. Now
she's grown up to look just like her mom: tall, graceful, beautiful,
and kind, and she had a family too. He thought it was ironic that
Rinda Blu's husband was white. It made Kevin smile inside.

Chapter 68

Daniel's Passing

A few years later, Rin's second husband, Daniel, passed away. She arranged for his money to be left to various charities and organizations they both supported throughout the world. And she began a variety of college scholarships in his name as well. Daniel and Rin talked about Kai quite often, and Rin saw him as often as she could. She kept up with Kai all these years; she loved him like he was one of her grandchildren. And by this time, Kai knew the real situation between Kevin and herself. She also knew that Kai was in contact with Kevin as well. Kai never talked about Kevin to Rin, and she was sure Kai gave no information about her to Kevin.

Rin only divulged to Daniel that she met Kai and his mother, Malia, on a visit to Hawaii. By the time Daniel passed away, Kai was finishing up with his undergraduate degree and applying to medical school. She knew Kevin had paid for all his undergraduate work and was planning to pay for medical school as well; Kai did tell her that. And Rin sent significant amounts of money to Kai and Malia every year to make things easier for them. Kai's father died a few years after he was born, so they could use the financial help. Nevertheless, Rin decided to use some of Daniel's scholarship money to help with Kai's medical school education.

She and Daniel didn't get married for his money; it was always about the companionship, respect, and friendship they had for each other. Although it might have seemed like a marriage of convenience, it was not. There was love, but not in the traditional sense between a man and woman; it could only be described like brother and sister. He was the big brother she never had. Rin wanted to protect Daniel somehow, as ironic as it sounds; he really had no one else as he became older, and he needed her.

Chapter 69

Rin's Visit to the Coffee Shop

After Daniel's passing, Rin retired completely from practicing law, and moved back to the States to live near her daughter, Rinda Blu. She moved into a beautiful three-bedroom condo just five miles away from where her daughter and family lived.

It was nearing the Thanksgiving holiday the year Rin returned, and Rinda Blu wanted her mother to stay with her family for at least a week. By this time, Rinda Blu's children were away at college, but they were coming home for the holidays. She missed her mom terribly and even though she lived only five miles away, she wanted her mom to spend those nights in her home, and to have a chance to enjoy the entire family.

Rin finally agreed and arrived with a small suitcase on the Tuesday before Thanksgiving so she could help Rinda Blu shop and prepare for the holiday dinner. Rin had to admit she was excited to spend time with her daughter, son-in-law, and grandchildren. It would be more of a celebration if Kai could have come for a visit as well. Rin was happy.

That Wednesday morning before Thanksgiving, the weather was beautiful. The sun was shining brightly, and the skies were pure blue. There were no clouds, and the winds blew calmly and softly. It was about 50 degrees and all Rin needed was a warm enough coat to get out and enjoy the weather. After breakfast, Rin told her daughter she wanted to take a walk, do some early Christmas shopping, and would return in a few hours. Rinda Blu's home was located near a small upscale downtown shopping corridor, so it was a convenient outing for Rin. As she was leaving, her daughter shouted, "mom please be careful, and don't stay too long or I'll come looking for you." Rin smiled and waved as she opened the front door to leave.

During her walk, Rin again reflected on Kevin as she did many times throughout her life. She found herself in front of the coffee shop where Rinda Blu said she had met Kevin; and he asked her daughter to give her his phone number. Rin just couldn't bring herself to call him, but she missed him more than ever. She didn't know if the coffee shop was her true destination, or she just happened to come across it. But there she was standing completely still in front, looking in. She stood there for a few moments and slowly walked away, but then turned quickly to go in. Rin stood inside the front door staring at the coffee shop's décor. She whispered to herself, "what a lovely place." She found herself in the customer line to be served. It was a little crowded, but most people were taking their orders to go, so there were a few empty tables available.

Rin ordered a hot coffee with pumpkin spice and cream which was the special for the holidays. She sat down at one of the smaller empty tables and took off her coat to get comfortable. She then took a sip of her coffee and marveled at how good it was. She sat there for a half hour tuning out the noise around her. She only thought about Kevin and his visit with Rinda Blu at that very spot. After the final sip of coffee, Rin checked her phone for the time, put on her coat, and grabbed her purse to leave that wonderful little place. After she left, she turned back to look once more, and continued her walk.

Kevin was getting ready to take that 30-minute drive to the coffee shop where he first met Rin's daughter. He visited that same place quite often; at least two or three times a week. He only happened to stop there that first day because of business nearby, and just happened to see Rin's lovely daughter; the daughter they should have had together. The one-hour drive both ways didn't matter to Kevin, maybe one day he would run into Rinda Blu again and hear more about her mother.

But this day, Kevin left a little later than usual. As he grabbed his car keys and headed through his kitchen to the back door; he received a phone call from his oldest Son, Brian, and sat down at his kitchen table to speak with him. Kevin was close to all three of his sons, but Brian spoke with him nearly every day and visited him quite often. During the conversation, Brian asked, "dad why didn't you ever marry again? You know mom would have wanted you to be happy." Kevin responded, "I don't know son, just haven't found the right gal."

Brian continued, "it's because of your Rin, right? We talked about her." Kevin said, "I don't want to talk about this now son, let's talk later. I have an errand to run." Brian continued anyway, "you're headed to that coffee shop, right? 30-minutes just to have a cup of coffee. It makes no sense, Dad." Kevin responded, "It's just something I must do. Let's talk later, I said." Kevin quickly hung up the phone, he didn't want to continue the conversation.

Tragically, on this exceptionally beautiful day, Kevin arrived at the coffee shop a little later than usual, and just three minutes after Rin left to continue her walk and do some shopping.

Chapter 70

Rin's Transition Begins

More years passed by, and Rin was in her early eighties by this time. When Rin was eighty-two years old, she became very ill. She had always been healthy, with lots of vitality, and she was still very beautiful. It was unusual for her to be sick, except for the occasional migraine headache and seasonal cold. Her doctors said there was no reason for her illness; there was nothing they could find that was causing her to be this sick. It was almost like she was ready to go, just giving up. Rinda Blu thought this was not like her mom; there must be something medically wrong, there must be. The doctors ran all kinds of tests but couldn't find anything.

It was time for Rin to make her transition. Rinda Blu called Kai immediately. He had been a doctor for a while now; he might be able to help. Kai said he would be there as soon as possible. Rinda Blu could hear Kai's voice breaking on the phone.

On the day of Rin's transition, she told her daughter about her secret, the man she loved nearly her entire life; his name was Kevin. It was the man she met in the coffee shop all those years ago. She told her daughter as much as she could about the wonderful love they had for each other. It had become difficult for Rin to talk by this time. Rinda Blu instantly remembered Kevin, recalling how heartbroken he seemed when he learned Rin had married again. Thank God she saved Kevin's phone number; something compelled her to do so. She decided to call him. Maybe he could see her mother before she died. Rinda Blu was very upset, not sure what to do; she was losing her mom, her best friend, the most beautiful woman in the world in Rinda Blu's eyes. Maybe she could make her happy this one last time by finding Kevin.

She told her mom that she would find Kevin for her, just to hold on until she could see him again.

Rin said, "No worries, my Baby Blu. Kevin is already waiting for me in the next lifetime."

Blu didn't understand, but she was frantic to find Kevin, so she made that call.

A man answered the phone; she said, "May I speak with Kevin?"

The man said, "Who is this?"

Rinda Blu said, "My name is Rin, my mom is Katherine, an old friend of Kevin. May I please speak with him? It's very important."

The man said sadly, "My name is Brian, and Kevin was my father. He talked about Rin all the time and how much he loved her; she was on his mind before he died. Would that be you?"

"Died?" Blu cried. "When?"

Brian said, "I'm sorry to say my father passed away about three days ago. Are you the Rin he talked about? I believe my dad died of a broken heart. You broke my father's heart."

Rinda Blu was astounded; she could barely speak. "Your father must have called my mother Rin as well, and that's why she named me Rinda. Please know my mother loved your father very much and had her reasons for not being with him; they had to be very good reasons. She would have never left someone she loved as much as your dad if it wasn't for a very good reason. I'm so very sorry for your loss. I really am. I fear I will lose my mother as well before this day ends."

Rinda Blu hung up the phone. She realized her mother had become ill exactly three days ago, when Kevin passed.

Chapter 71

Rin's Passing

She went back to her mom's side and looked at the ring she wore on her right hand; she remembered the ring Kevin kissed in the coffee shop. She asked her mom if Kevin gave her that ring. Rin said yes, in a faint voice. Rinda Blu recalled her mom's visit to the island some thirty years ago; that's when the ring suddenly appeared. She wore that ring every day and rarely took it off. After that trip, her mom seemed sad all the time. She had a good life, but there was something missing that Rinda Blu couldn't put her finger on. But now she realized, it must have been Kevin; what could have happened between them? Why didn't she tell her about him? She must have had a good reason. But it was too late to know now, and she didn't press her for more information. It was her mom's secret, and that was okay.

Rinda Blu watched as her mother's breaths grew more labored; she recalled asking her mother some years ago why she divorced her father. Her mother and father were such good friends after the divorce; her mother even seemed to like her dad's new wife very much. They all got along so well; Rinda Blu just couldn't understand why they got divorced.

Her mom said her father was an exceptionally good man, and he loved his daughter very much. Rin initially didn't want the divorce; she wanted to stay together, in part, because of Rinda Blu. Her mother couldn't even explain to herself why she wanted to stay married to Robert. Maybe it was easier than being single. But he deserved so much more than what she was able to give him. He deserved a special kind of happiness between a husband and wife: passion, spirituality, and that beautiful love and joy that comes with it. He found that unconditional love with his new wife, and that was why her mom liked her.

Rin also said Robert always thought something was missing in their marriage, and he was right; the missing piece was her feelings for him. She just couldn't love him in the way he wanted; she tried but couldn't, and she hated herself for that. But Rinda Blu was a result of their union; she was a gift that brought her so much joy. Rinda Blu was her greatest achievement in life. So, God makes no mistakes. When Robert asked for a divorce, she didn't fight him; it was amicable. She agreed to everything he wanted during the divorce proceedings; he was fair. All she wanted was to raise her Baby Blu as the primary parent.

Rin went on to say, "Your dad contributed to God's gift that brought me such a beautiful and wonderful daughter, and I will be forever grateful to Robert for that."

Rinda Blu's father always told her, "You are your mom's pride and joy; you are her dear Baby Blu, the most important person in the world to her."

Now Rinda Blu wondered if Kevin was the second most important person, keeping in mind that her mom tried to always put God first.

The fact that her mom was dying brought about the most pain Rinda Blu had ever experienced. Her mom brought so much happiness to others, always putting others before herself. The happiness and needs of others are what drove her throughout her life. Her mom put Rinda Blu and her family first, with every thought and decision she made in her life. It was her mom's generosity and empathy for those less fortunate that defined her throughout her life. She had given so much of herself and expected little; so many people loved her. She was beyond wonderful; she was a magnificent human being. She is the best mother anyone could ever have, a tremendous example to her and her children.

She feared Kai wouldn't make it in time. She wanted her mom to see him before her transition; they were very close, and that would make her very happy. Rinda Blu also believed Kai knew all about Kevin; he knew more about her mother's secret. In stands to reason because Kai was born on Lanai. But one thing was for sure: Her mother loved Kai very much.

Rinda Blu recalled her mother's belief in God and a life that is promised after someone passes away. Her mother taught her about God's beautiful place that we go to in the next lifetime, where there is serenity and contentment, and there is no pain.

She believed as her mother did, and with tears in her eyes, Rinda Blu said, "Mom, it's all okay. I'll be okay, and your grandchildren will be okay. Kevin is waiting for you. I know how much he loved you, and I'm so happy you'll be together again. He's waiting for you in the next lifetime."

Rin smiled and said, "I know, my sweet Baby Blu," and closed her eyes while taking her last breath of life on this earth.

As her eyes filled with more tears, Rinda Blu looked at her beautiful mother and thought, *Even at eighty-two years of age, my mother is absolutely stunning. How will I go on without her?* But a smile soon came to her face and within her heart, so she whispered, "Dear God, my mother has gone home, and Kevin, please take care of her."

Chapter 72

In the Next Lifetime

R in said many times to herself, if something happened to Kevin, she would know it, and she would surely die too. She could not stay on this earth if something happened to him. She always told Kevin, "Baby, I'll be with you in the next lifetime," something she believed with all her heart and soul. She believed God would ensure it. Kevin and Rin had made mistakes by being together, but in the last thirty years, Rin tried to make up for those mistakes for them both by refusing to see him. She wanted God to forgive them both.

Rin helped Kevin understand that regardless of religion or your personal experience with death, they would share an afterlife. Heaven was an infinite world of new discoveries for them. Rin often quoted Thomas Boston, who said, "The divine perfections will be an unbounded field, in which the glorified shall walk eternally, seeing more and more of God, since they can never come to the end of the infinite." God would forgive those stolen moments they expressed their love and the times they spent together if they only asked for his forgiveness. And Rin asked God every day for that forgiveness for them both.

Kevin was indeed waiting for Rin in the most beautiful place imaginable. He looked the same as when they were on the island of Lanai, Hawaii. Rin came walking toward him, looking the same as well. Kevin reminded her of when she saw him in the villa in Lanai, gazing at the beautiful view. Rin was dressed in a long off-white linen sun dress and wore flat white sandals; she appeared to Kevin like a beautiful angel. He was reminded of how Rin just took his breath away. As Rin walked toward Kevin in this beautiful place, music entered her mind, Deniece Williams' version of the old spiritual, "God Is Amazing." She looked at Kevin, that wonderful man she loved so much. The music filled her with joy and peace; Rin was so happy.

Kevin smiled as she came toward him. He said, "I love you, babe, and I've missed you so much. You always said in the next lifetime. We're finally here, together, and it's forever."

Tears came to Rin; she never felt so much joy and happiness. It was a state of fulfillment and contentment that could not be described; it was God's gift and God's embrace of them both. Kevin put his arms around her, and she laid her head on his shoulder.

Rin whispered, "Forever, sweetheart."

They stood next to the beautiful tree in Maui, where Kevin had carved their names. Rin thought for a moment; did this gorgeous tree survive the devastating fires in Maui, or was this an image, another gift from God? It didn't matter, of course; God had, indeed, forgiven them both.

In the Next Lifetime

Rin's Love Poem to Kevin

We come from a different place, a different space, in this time.
But our love and hopes for a future have made us nearly blind.

How could I notice you, want you, and crave your perfect touch?
I live in this fog of existence; my body aches for you so very much.

From the first time we kissed, I knew you loved me, and I loved you.
I'm lost in your kindness, your spirit, your gentleness, and your
eyes so blue.

Your joy, your success, and protection in this life are all I ever
wanted.
Giving you up hurts me so bad, it's so painful, and I'm haunted.

In the beginning, before we went our separate ways and married
others,
We did not fight for our existence in this world; we did not fight
our brothers.

Some say we should be together like black coffee with lots of cream.
Others say, "No! No!" Our union would be a nightmare invading
a dream.

You've given me passion as you lay against what you call my
caramel-colored skin.
And oh, how I smile, when you give me that sheepish grin.

Our attraction is beyond physical beauty; it's a spiritual connection
of our hearts.
We've made mistakes; God will understand and forgive us when
we depart.

It's very funny; you were not my type and not part of my world.
We are so different, it scared me at first; my life became twisted
and swirled.

So I say goodbye for now, my love; it is for us both I ask God's
forgiveness.
I love you, I do love you, always and forever, in this existence.

We both understand our lives are not our own.
It is in the next lifetime, we'll be together and call heaven our home.

It is in the next lifetime, where there is no sorrow, that I'll see you
again.
It is in the next lifetime, a place of peace, where our love will be
ordained.
It is in the next lifetime, the kingdom of heaven, together, we will
attain.

About Lanai

K evin and Rin are fictional characters who spent twelve days
on the island of Lanai, Hawaii. Later in the book, they took a
ferry ride from Lanai to Maui. In August 2023, the historic town of
Lahaina, on Maui, suffered deadly wildfires that killed hundreds of
people and forced thousands to evacuate. The tragedy was fueled by
a mix of land and atmospheric conditions that created fire weather.
This massive blaze destroyed much of the town of Lahaina, and the
devastation from the loss of life and the destruction of the town's
beauty were heartbreaking. This shattered the lives of those who
lived there; our thoughts and prayers are with them for generations.
The fictional characters of Kai and his mother, Malia, lived on the
island of Lanai, which was spared the destruction.

Although Lanai has only a few options for outdoor adventure,
Kevin and Rin had their adventures. While Lanai is notorious for its
quiet, unspoiled, and pristine atmosphere, there is plenty of action
and adventure to explore. Kevin and Rin had their adventures and
close calls; however, Lania proved to be a place to slow down and
unwind, while also getting your feet dirty with endless hiking and
off-road options. The very walkable Lanai City is also home to good
eateries and much more.

Ten Amazing Facts about Lanai

1. At just over 140 square miles, Lanai is the sixth largest island of the Hawaiian Island chain. According to the 2023 Census, Lanai has 3,164 residents. The five largest ethnic groups in Lanai City are Asian (non-Hispanic: 51.4%), white (non-Hispanic: 16.6%), two or more groups (non-Hispanic: 15.9%), Native Hawaiian and Other Pacific Islander (non-Hispanic: 8.12%), and white (Hispanic: 3.13%).

2. Legend has it that Lanai was once inhabited by man-eating spirits until a Maui prince, Kaulua'au, was sent to the island as punishment by his father for pulling up a bread tree. The king expected his son to die on the island. Instead, the prince flourished and drove the spirits away. As a reward, he was given control of the island.

3. The origin of the name Lanai is not known. The island was often referred to by its full name, Lanai o Kaulua'au. In a nod to the Maui prince, the translation is "day of the conquest of Kaulua'au."

4. The first inhabitants of Lanai were thought to be from Maui and Molokai. They established fishing villages along the coastline but were nearly all wiped out when King Kamehameha united the eight Hawaiian islands with an iron fist.

5. In 1921, the first pineapple was planted on Lanai. Charles Dole bought the island for the sole purpose of growing pineapples. Lanai soon acquired the nickname the Pineapple Island. By 1930, the tiny island was exporting over 65,000 tons of pineapple a year. The final harvest of pineapple

on Lanai occurred in 1992. People still refer to it as the Pineapple Island.

6. Hawaii became a US territory in 1898 and became the fiftieth state in August 1959, following a referendum in which more than 93 percent of Hawaiians approved the proposition that the territory should be admitted as a state.

7. There are no traffic lights on Lanai. Lanai High and Elementary School, which educates children from kindergarten through twelfth grade, is the only school on the island. And there is only one hospital.

8. Lanai has some of the best snorkeling in the entire state of Hawaii.

9. Oracle Software founder and billionaire Larry Ellison owns 98 percent of the island, while Hawaii owns the other 2 percent. Ellison also owns nearly one-third of all the housing (the state owns the rest) and pretty much every other business on the island, including two Four Seasons hotels. He also spent millions refurbishing the island's lone movie theater and constructing a resort-style Olympic-sized public pool. He worked with the state to update the water filtration system in Lanai City and built a domestic violence center for women.

10. While snorkeling is the main attraction on Lanai, the island has three golf courses, two affiliated with the Four Seasons resorts and a free, nine-hole course. Fun fact: Bill Gates was married on one of the Four Seasons courses.

To the Reader

I hope you enjoyed reading about the beauty and splendor of love between Kevin and Rin, no matter how imperfect and tragic. The island of Lanai and its magnificence is where they had an opportunity to express their love further and get some questions answered from their past. These images from the island will help you imagine this place of serenity and how it enhanced their time together.

CC Lane